To Ray —

my favorite keyboard player!

Enjoy

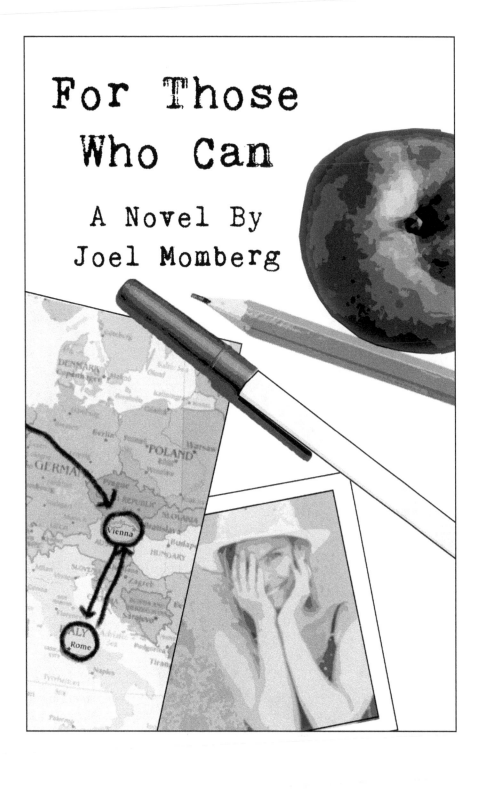

For Those Who Can

A Novel By
Joel Momberg

Copyright © 2020 by Joel Momberg

Published by Born Young Publishers
P.O. Box 7161
St. Petersburg, FL 33734
www.iwasbornveryyoung.com

For information about the author and to order his books, go to
www.joelmomberg.com.

ISBN 978-0-578-78771-8

"And you know that when the truth is told,
you can get what you want or you can just get old ....
When will you realize, Vienna waits for you?"

– Billy Joel
Vienna, 1977

This book is dedicated to:
Cole, Grace, Wyatt, Remy and Avery
(the Grands)

PREFACE

For *Those Who Can* is a love story.

It's about a teacher's love for his students, love between a man and a woman, love of friends and family and love of the legacies that others have left for us to follow. It's love in the truest form ... wonderful, scary, dangerous and messy.

I was a teacher for six years, three as a college preparatory teacher and three in the classroom. Some of the experiences that I detailed (admittedly) closely followed my early career.

The title of the book is one most teachers have unfortunately heard as a derogatory opening line of a quote that sometimes is used as a reference by others who scoff at what teachers do:

Those who can ... do / Those who can't ... teach.

For years, I had a coffee mug on my desk in response to that remark which simply read: Those who can ... TEACH.

This book was written For Those Who Can.

I truly loved teaching. The students were incredible; I learned so much from them. Many still contact me on social media and I love hearing from them.

This was a difficult year (2020). Covid-19 was the great interrupter that we all dealt with. I also was battling the effects of stage four melanoma of the liver and undergoing immunotherapy. There were days that I just didn't feel like writing. But by persisting, I feel that it was truly part of my healing process.

Special thanks to all those mentioned in the book who are real characters (you know who you are) who had such an impact on my life and to my great friend Dave Scheiber, who helped me along the way with advice and encouragement. He is and always will be one of the best writers I know.

And to my wife Debbie. I would not let her see any pages until I was through. She allowed me to again be selfish in the time I spent holed up on the beach or in my office at home writing this novel. She is such a tremendous support to me.

Thanks to friends and family who were always there.

I hope you enjoy *For Those Who Can.*

CONTENTS

PROLOGUE

Alan's Manuscript Appears.................................. 1

CHAPTER ONE

Meeting Karol Rae Ballard................................. 5

CHAPTER TWO

First Assignment: Tough Love 23

CHAPTER THREE

Indiana Wants Me.. 51

CHAPTER FOUR

Sadness and Elation..................................... 109

CHAPTER FIVE

Stuck in a Fellini Movie................................ 123

CHAPTER SIX

Vienna Waits For You.................................... 153

CHAPTER SEVEN

The Visit to Meridian 183

EPILOGUE

Jake Finds the Answers 189

PROLOGUE

Alan's Manuscript Appears

The assembled crowd at Beth Israel Cemetery, almost in unison, opened their collective umbrellas as Rabbi Harold Schulman concluded his remarks.

Jacob Handler didn't notice the rain. He stared, deep in thought, at the gravesite of his father, Alan. His uncle, Gary, raised his large black umbrella and moved closer to his distraught nephew as the rain now came down in sheets.

This time of year in New Orleans, it's not uncommon to see massive rain storms come quickly and disappear just as fast. Standing there in one of the oldest cemeteries in New Orleans, Jacob was transported back in time. Jacob, at 46, felt closer to 76 as the crowd started to disperse and he studied all of his father's friends in attendance. Beth Israel Cemetery is at the end of Canal Street where Metairie Road crosses, important to Alan and Jacob because that site was built on slightly higher ground at the Metairie Levee and it allowed for burials to be done in the ground – a very important tenet of the Jewish religion – to be buried below ground. Most of New Orleans, as is well known, sits well under sea level and many of the other cemeteries are built with gravesites that sit above ground. Jake hoped this was where his father wanted to be. They never really discussed it in detail other than a casual remark or two that he made at dinner about following tradition when he passed away. Jake's mother wanted to be cremated and that created some friction in the family, but of course, his father conceded. She was Catholic.

Now they are both gone.

Both were taken way too soon, thought Jake. A tragic helicopter accident, while they enjoyed a much-needed vacation in Hawaii just days before, ended the lives of both his parents.

"Jake, are you riding with us?" Gary Handler said as he put his arm around his nephew.

"I think I might just stay for a little while longer, Uncle Gary."

Gary's son Freddie handed Jacob his umbrella. "Here, Jake. I'll share Dad's and we will send the car back for you."

"Thanks, Freddie." The rain started to relent as the cemetery cleared out quickly. Jacob stood in silence, remembering his dad. He was a larger-than-life man, a best-selling novelist, successful screenwriter, entrepreneur and educator. He had so many friends and so many stories were told about him.

"Excuse me. You're Jacob, correct?" the only other remaining mourner in the cemetery approached and asked. Jacob didn't recognize him. He was likely in his 70s, Jacob thought; he wore very thick glasses and looked a little like Albert Einstein, only heavier. And much shorter. "So very sorry for your loss ... a great loss for all of us. I'm Emory Ohlmstead. I was your father's attorney and close friend for over 40 years."

Jacob shook hands. "Emory, huh? Don't know anybody else named Emory. Except you and me. Emory's my middle name, Jacob Emory Handler."

Emory smiled. "Jacob, I have something for you. Your father wanted you to have this." He held out a manuscript box. "It's his last manuscript. It was never published. It's actually a partial autobiography. He had me hold this until he passed. I think you'll find it very interesting. There are things in here that you probably never knew about your dad."

Jacob looked at the box, then at Emory. He was almost afraid to touch it. "When did he write this?"

"He wrote it a few years ago." Emory held it out and Jacob took it in his arms. "It's unfinished, unfortunately. I just want you to know that if you ever need me for anything or have any questions, you can always call me."

Emory handed Jake his business card. He glanced at it. "South Bend, Indiana?"

"Yes. We have offices in Indianapolis as well but that's where you'll find me."

"Thanks," Jake said as he glanced at the card again, "Mr. Ohlmstead."

"So happy to have finally met the other Emory," he winked.

By the time Jacob arrived at his house, there were still about 50 or so relatives and friends paying their respects. Jacob talked to them all and gradually disappeared into the bedroom, totally exhausted. He fell into bed.

At four in the morning, he woke up to find that he still had all his clothes on. He was hugging the manuscript box that Emory had handed him and took it to his desk.

As much information as there was about Alan Handler,

there were always missing pieces of his life for Jacob. He knew very little about his history, grandparents, almost everything before he was born.

Jacob carefully opened the box and read the title page: *For Those Who Can...* by Alan Handler.

He turned to chapter one ...

CHAPTER ONE

Meeting Karol Rae Ballard

Karol Rae Ballard came into my life on July 14, 1974 and changed it forever. Like most life-changing moments, I had no clue at the time. But even in my 24-year-old underdeveloped, adolescent mind, there was something different about that day.

Truth be told, I almost missed my own destiny. I had written down the wrong address of READInc, the company I had just signed up with – housed in the building where Karol Rae Ballard sat perched in row three, seat four. Frantically, I checked the phonebook. There was a number listed but no street address. I walked around Canal Boulevard without success two or three times.

Finally, a little man sitting at the bus stop reading his paper pointed to a tiny sign above the flower shop: "READInc Educational Services." I thanked him profusely. I think I scared him a little as he shrunk away from me while I shook his hand a little too hard.

I was late.

Opening the door to the flower shop was a little surreal. All I could think about was that this was either a front for some crazy mafioso biz or there would be nothing there but a sign and a locked door.

I was wrong on both accounts, fortunately.

The back of the store opened to a hallway that was deceptively large. At the center was a large brass elevator welcoming me to my new career and my new life. I stepped inside and pushed the button for the second floor (the only other floor) and waited interminably for the elevator door to open.

There it was. The READInc main office greeted me as I stepped out. Big wooden and glass doors opened to a pretty comfortable couch with a very friendly receptionist who, thankfully, recognized my name.

"Well, Mr. Handler, your class is awaiting; right through those doors on the right," she said as she handed me a large notebook.

"Thanks," I said. "They started already?"

"Yes. About 10 minutes ago."

I hesitated for a minute, not sure whether to knock or just bust in.

I did both.

"Come on in," said Tommy Thompson, the company COO momentarily, as he stopped his opening remarks. "You're Alan Handler, right?"

"Yes sir. Sorry I'm late. Got a little lost, " I stammered.

"No problem. Just have a seat. There's a desk right over here."

Row three, seat four. Two seats down from row three, seat two. And there she was ... the shiksa goddess. I thought I was in one of those romcoms where the girl does the slow-motion turn and her long blonde hair floats across her back.

Karol Rae Ballard. She was stunning.

Seriously, the light from the slightly opened window

blinds hit her eyes in a perfect angle and created a bright blue piercing image that I couldn't turn away from.

"Mr. Handler?" Thompson said for the second time.

"Huh?"

"I was just asking if you'd like to say a few words about yourself."

"No. Um, that's okay."

"Was a rhetorical question. We would like to know about you."

Shit. I hate this part. I never liked presenting stuff – especially about myself.

"Well, let's see. I was born very young ..."

A few chuckles around the room. That joke in the beginning seems to help.

"... and I live here in New Orleans. Went to LSU and worked in an ad agency for a year. Saw an ad in the paper about this job. Teach, travel to new places and meet new people. Sounded great to me."

"We are happy you joined us." Thompson said and the class politely clapped. "Okay let's continue on page 12 of your notebooks."

Crap, I guess I missed all the other intros in the class. Especially you know who. She was focused on Thompson now, turning her attention to every word. And I was totally focused on her. What the hell, I can read the notebook and catch up later. There must be a break or something coming up. Lunch? That's it! I'll see where she's going for lunch.

Suddenly the room went silent. I looked around and everyone was writing. I strained to see what the assignment was as I thumbed through the notebook. This is great, I thought I'd already messed up ...

"The questionnaire in the front of the notebook, Handler." A voice hoarsely whispered on my left. It belonged to a huge guy with a crewcut. "He wants us to fill out the teaching experience now."

"Thanks ..." I looked at him.

"Miley," He said. "Phil Miley. Oh and by the way, I heard she's engaged."

I frowned and pointed my head toward Karol Ballard in a questioning way.

"Yeah."

"That sucks," I said a little too loud. She heard it and smiled.

Thompson stood in the middle of the classroom and said, "Okay. When you finish filling those out, bring them up front and then you are free to go. Short day today. I've got to call a few schools this afternoon. So ... we will start again bright and early tomorrow."

I didn't have too much left to fill out since I had no experience, so I gathered up my stuff, stood and handed my form to Mr. Thompson. Just when I turned to ask Karol her name, Thompson tapped my shoulder. "Mr. Handler, can we meet in my office?"

I looked around and she had already headed out the door.

Thompson's office was mostly bookshelves and a wooden desk. He apparently didn't sit a lot. His desk chair was nowhere to be seen. I sat in the corner on the only chair in the room. He perched on the corner of his desk.

"So, Alan ... Can I call you that?"

"Sure."

"I see you have no teaching experience."

I looked around then stared at the floor. "No, I don't. I told Mr. Dingly that when I applied."

"And he probably said 'no problem,' right?"

"He did." I started to feel tiny sweat drops on my forehead. "Is there a problem?"

Thompson smiled. "Not really. I just want you to be aware that you will have a different instructional track from some of the others in class and depending how well you do in training ... you may be assigned differently from some of the teachers who have had experience."

"How many others are like me?"

"None."

I was stunned. Everyone else who got this job had some teaching experience? "Was there a mistake?"

"Nope," said Thompson, " Dingley saw something in you that he liked. Half the battle is class management and having a relatable personality to high school kids. He saw that in you. He told me. I'll teach you the rest. This program is not traditional curriculum. There's a prescribed way to teach it." I must have had fear splashed across my face at this point. He saw it. "Didn't mean to scare you Mr. Handler. You'll do fine. I promise you that. But if by the end of the training you feel that it's not for you, or I think you can't hack it, we will part ways. Okay?"

"Okay."

It was about seven o'clock when I climbed into my usual barstool at Charlie's and hoisted up my new READInc notebook. After my meeting with Thompson, I decided I should read as much as I could quickly and the best way to get through it was with a Dixie beer or two or three.

July in New Orleans was brutal. Even at night you could feel the sweat dripping off your body as soon as you stepped outside. Charlie's was just a few blocks from my apartment on Conti and was open to the elements. It was a little brighter than most local bars. Instead of long and narrow with no windows, the bar was raised and centered close to a few good-size windows.

"Anything else I can get for you before I head out?" the bartender, Lexi, asked.

"What's in the bottle that's on the top shelf?" I asked, squinting at a bottle of Belvedere.

"It's the stuff you never order and you probably can't pronounce."

"Can I take a look?"

"Sure, Handler, just get your big ass over here and shimmy up the ladder and take a look."

Busted. I knew she wouldn't do it. And she knew why I did. Lexi had a kick-ass body and great legs and just watching her climb that ladder is worth the price of another drink.

"It's Belvedere, asshole!" From behind me I heard his voice and dreaded turning around. It was Brian Johnson. He was either stoned or drunk or worse – neither. I hated when he came in.

"Handler, you sorry sack of shit. You are sitting here by yourself reading from a notebook?"

"Don't you have someone else you can piss off tonight?" I barked. "Maybe there's a group of nuns drinking wine in the corner somewhere." Brian grabbed me around my shoulders from behind and tried to knock my notebook off the bar.

I still hadn't turned around when another voice scolded him. "Hey Brian, that's a valuable book. Don't you mess with that. I have one just like it and I carry it everywhere."

That's when he let go so that I could turn and see the one and only KAROL RAE BALLARD! What the hell? Of all the gin joints, in all the towns in all the world, she walks into mine. I could have said that. I could have been cool and used a Casablanca reference but no … I said, "Hey."

"Hey," she answered back.

Silence. I sat there stunned trying to think of clever conversation but nothing.

"Karol. Wait," Brian said. "You know Handler?"

"Haven't officially met but he's in my training class at my new job."

I stood up and held out my hand. "Karol, huh? I'm Alan. Alan Handler."

She smiled and took my hand. Brian jumped in and interrupted, of course. "He's in your class? Handler?" Turning to address me, "I thought you had a future at the Wendy's drive thru."

"That was in high school, putz."

Karol smiled. "Brian is a putz. He's also my cousin."

"That's good," I wiped my forehead. "I thought you might have chosen to be with him as a friend."

Brian had drifted off to order three beers from Lexi.

"Well, I have to say that I'm grateful to him for giving me a place to live while I'm here in New Orleans."

"That's generous of him. Where are you from?"

"Mississippi."

"What a small world. Running into you here." So much I wanted to ask her. I wanted to separate her from Brian as soon as possible so I could talk.

Brian came back and handed me a cold one. He toasted us after he gave Karol hers. "Okay, okay. Let's think of a toast. Um ... To old friends, new friends, cousins ... people of New Orleans who come to the Quarter to drink and to laugh and to ..."

"Shut up, Brian. Cheers," Karol said and clinked glasses.

I definitely liked her.

Fortunately, Brian caught the eye of a brunette who was standing (barely) down the bar from us. He winked and she smiled. He flopped an arm over my shoulder. "If you two will excuse me. I seem to have an unscheduled appointment with that young lady that I MUST attend to."

"Thank God she doesn't have her glasses on." He grabbed his beer and was gone.

Breaking the ice with Karol was not at all as difficult as I thought it would be. In fact it was easy. She was so open and honest that I almost felt at times like she was trusting me with personal information that I was too privileged to receive. And I accepted the responsibility of not misusing it.

She was also a little buzzed ... as was I.

Karol was born in Meridian, Mississippi and spent her childhood there. She had an abusive father with a drinking problem who was well educated and worked a series of sales jobs that put him on the road a lot. He died while she was in middle school. Karol's mom was a kindergarten teacher and was blessed with great patience, as Karol told it.

The oldest of two children, her younger brother Kelly was manic depressive. He still lived at home and was very close to Karol as she was the one who helped raise him.

"So how did you wind up here?" I asked her.

"Needed a change."

"So you chose READInc?"

"Not right away. I chose New Orleans. Closest escape point for a quick getaway. There was a guy." She laughed at herself. "Always a guy. His name is Andy. Met him at college. I was getting a psychology degree and he was a grad assistant." She stopped there and took a long sip of her beer and looked down.

"Hey Handler. What about you? I've been running my mouth forever and you haven't told me anything."

"What do you wanna know?"

"Do you believe in God?"

I sat up straight. That was the last question I expected. I was ready with my autobiography and that zinger hit.

"Sure. I believe there's a God."

"A God? Like Jesus?"

"Not him but God … for sure."

"So you're one of those guys that killed him, huh?"

I was stunned.

She continued laughing. "Relax. I knew you were Jewish. Andy's Jewish too and you kind of remind me of him."

"That's a good thing?"

"Not good or bad. Just … a thing. I'm a little Southern shiksa." She struck a pose with her hand folded in prayer.

"That's a thing that no longer defines me but it's part of who I am."

"Are you really a Mississippi girl?"

"Expected different, huh? Thought when I said Mississippi I would bat my eyes and give you a long drawn out southern 'I doooo declare'?"

"Well ... yes." I cracked up at her impression of a Mississippi girl. "Went to LSU with a bunch of girls from Mississippi and you are definitely different."

"Okay, your turn now. I'll try to not interrupt. What's your story, Mr. Handler?"

This was the part where I try to make my life sound much more interesting than it is. I'm always trying to impress whoever I'm addressing so I embellish parts of my story that I think are boring. Not sure I'll get away with doing that with Karol. She seems to be pretty adept at figuring out bullshit.

I started with the basics. Growing up in New Orleans with a neurotic Jewish mother, and a dad who died young ... we managed to get by.

Karol interrupted briefly, "That sucks. It must have been hard to lose your father so young."

"My older brother kept us all grounded. I think. He became like a substitute father."

I told Karol that music and art were my passions. Here is where I drifted a little and embellished some. I really did love both but if they were my passions I would have worked harder on them. I majored in graphic design at LSU (after trying architecture, marketing and business). It took me an extra year to finish my B.A. I worked for an ad agency locally doing paste-up work and some creative but mostly grunt work for the REAL artists. I was bored.

That's when I discovered READInc.

"So are you married?" Karol asked out of the blue. "Sorry, I said I would shut up."

"No. I'm not married." I answered. "But you are about to be, right?"

"What makes you say that?"

"Word has it among your classmates that you are engaged."

Karol tilted her head back and laughed loudly. "No. Not even close. I spread that rumor when guys hit on me." There was another pregnant pause as Karol sipped her beer. I started to change the subject but she continued. "Andy ... the guy I was telling you about ... had asked me to marry him. Fortunately, I didn't. Great guy. He had so many sweet qualities. But he fucked up his life and mine. Alcohol will do that you know? Changes your whole personality. He just ... changed. And I didn't. So I got fed up. Still young, not engaged, so bye-bye blues. Right?" She held up her glass and we toasted.

Brian came back right around that time. "Hey ... are you ready to roll?" he asked Karol.

"What about your friend?"

"Her husband just got here. He wasn't pleased with my invitation to party."

Karol nodded and put down her beer. "Mr. Handler. See you in class." Then whispered, "Unless I scared you away."

"Not at all. I will definitely see you in class."

God, I like her.

My head felt like a big ball of cotton the next day. It hurt to even look at the pages of my notebook. But there was Karol two seats down looking refreshed and attentive. She peered over her shoulder and gave me a wink.

Tommy Thompson liked to move around when he talked. Today it was down one row and up another then encircling the room. To me it was very distracting. I liked to look at the speaker and with him that was impossible.

"Our company was founded on the premise that all students should have an equal shot at a college education," he began. "David Dingley, our founder and CEO, was singleminded in this premise. When he designed the curriculum that you'll be studying over the next two weeks he tested it and refined it on thousands of students over the last 10 years. Every day, we hear success stories from students and families from all over the world."

I looked at Phil Miley next to me and he was just beaming like he had discovered the cure for cancer. Phil, I found out later, was a country boy from Bogalusa who really wanted to be a teacher. He was on scholarship at LSU as a placekicker but was the unfortunate recipient of a compound fracture that ended his football career. Not one to complain or dwell on the negative, Phil took that as a sign from God to pursue his lifelong dream of teaching.

"Some of you might be asking 'Just how are we getting these kids into college?'" Thompson continued. "Well, we are giving them the tools to succeed and showing them how to use them. If they know how to comprehend what they read, if they can do it faster than most, if they understand how to take the SAT test, how to make their college application rise to the top of the stack ... they are light years ahead of their competitors."

Karol raised her hand.

Thompson: "Yes, Ms. Ballard. You have a question?"

Karol: "What about grades? If these kids don't have the grades to get in ... how are we gonna help them?"

Thompson, "Great question! The answer to that is of course we can't help everyone. We discuss options with parents in the initial orientation."

The "orientation" that Thompson referred to was where the underachieving students were weeded out. READInc sold the program to private/independent schools only and then tested everyone at the school for "free" to show parents where they fall in achievement levels. The interested parents then pay for their kids to take the course and we get assigned to those schools to teach it.

The course is taught in a series of 30-minute sessions (20 of them) and the school schedules the students according to how their other classes fall. Sometimes the course would be early morning, sometimes during the day and sometimes in the evenings for boarding schools. If we teach three times a week, the course runs about two months.

Dingley had a pretty good plan. The company was making lots of money on this program. Each student paid about $300 to enroll. We were paid nominal salaries, didn't work that hard and traveled to new places every few months. Independent schools didn't have the same restrictions that public schools had and were flexible with hours.

When we broke for lunch, I offered Karol a burger and a Barqs root beer at the neighboring Frostop. She couldn't refuse.

"So what did you think about that session?" I asked her.

"I think it's a bunch of bullshit but I'm ready to get started."

"You mean the part about the grades and weeding out the kids?"

"No. I mean the whole program. It's a way for those fat cats to make money and if it works, fine. If not … so what? Just a bunch of spoiled rotten private school brats who will get into college with daddy's money anyway."

I took a big bite of my burger and let this set in. Karol has a psychology degree. She's also obviously got a social conscience. There was a disconnect here. Why is she doing this job if she feels this way and could obviously be doing something else?

"But you're gonna still do it … right?"

"Right."

"Because …"

"Because it's a good job, I can be independent and … just because! Are you finished with your burger? Can we go?" Karol was now visibly angry.

"Hey, I'm sorry if I ask too many questions."

"Let's just go. I'm not hungry any more." She stood up and grabbed her trash.

"No. Wait. Sit down for a minute. I just want to understand."

"Understand what? Why I think this is a corporate scam but still accepted the job? You know, I was accepted into law school when I graduated. If I chose that path, I'd probably be defending Dingle or Schmingle or one of his contemporaries. So for now I'll just settle for the easier path and suck it up." She leaned in my direction. "What about you, Handler? Is this your dream job?"

"My dream job? No. But my options are a little more limited. I can cut and paste pictures of toilet paper for the newspaper and maybe learn to say 'Would you like fries with that?' Or teach kids for now." I finished off my root beer. "You know the guy next guy me? Phil? He's as happy as a pig in shit with all of this. I admire him. He knows exactly what he wants to do."

Karol reached over and whispered, "Thanks for the burger …" Then she kissed me and said, "I'm sorry I got so bitchy. Want a home cooked meal … tonight?"

Karol and I were inseparable after that. Over the next two weeks, we did everything together, knowing that as soon as we were given our assignments, our time together would be limited. My first assignment was already on the books: Camden, South Carolina. I had to start in three days. Karol didn't have one yet.

She was also about to face a new challenge.

Karol shared with me that her brother Kelly was not well. He had decided not to take his medications. No one discovered that he made that decision over a month earlier.

Karol's mother Sarah doted on her son. She excused his moods and personality swings as just quirky behavior. After all, she would say, he's got a brilliant mind and very little patience for ignorant people.

Karol's dark moods concerned me. I never thought that she was manic depressive or had any mental disorder. But I suspected that she thought she did. Or rather, she was deathly afraid that she might. She and Kelly were very close. When he called her –which was just about every day – she would get very quiet afterwards. I noticed that Karol had been drifting into some dark places from time to time.

The phone rang.

I could see in her eyes that it was not good. She took the phone and disappeared into the bathroom and I could hear her quietly sobbing.

"He's in the hospital," she managed to tell me as she finished her call. I put my arms around her. "He's okay, Mom said, but pretty fucked up."

"Go visit, Karol. You've got time before you get assigned and I know you'd feel better being there."

"You only have a couple of days left before you leave and I want to spend them here."

"No. You need to be home." We sat on the couch. "I can leave early to get settled. When I get a place, you can come stay with me in Camden … if Kelly's doing better, okay?"

I poured Karol a drink and brought it to her.

"Handler, I'm not sure I can do this anymore. My mom and Kelly and the whole thing you know?"

"Yes you can." I reached over and opened my notebook. "I almost forgot to tell you. I talked to Mr. Thompson about us, you know? And I said that our preference would be to travel to schools together if we could get large assignments that need two teachers or there are cities close together. He gave me a list of upcoming assignments and there are a few coming up. See?"

I handed her the list and pointed to a few.

"South Bend, Indiana has a large girls' school starting in a month or so and LaPorte has a boys' boarding school at the same time. They are only about 10 miles apart. You could take the girls and I'll take the boys. What do you think?"

"I think we make a pretty good team."

FOR THOSE WHO CAN

CHAPTER TWO

First Assignment: Tough Love

Nothing could prepare me for what I experienced at Miller Academy in Camden, South Carolina.

Thompson had given me a five-pager on the history of the school and the current state of affairs. It was established in the mid 1800s by Margaret Miller for African-American children of former slaves. It grew over the next 10 years to include living facilities for boys and girls. Interestingly, Mrs. Miller was a Quaker missionary from Massachusetts and the student population was largely from the Northeast.

The school produced notable alumni in its heyday but in recent years, it was in a decline. Student population for K-12 was 100 and rising costs had a negative impact on maintaining the campus.

I studied the map and the key contacts that morning as I sat down to breakfast in the Camden Motel, my new home for two months. The motel was clean and the food was actually very good. Finding a place to live for two months was a challenge. READInc gave every teacher a living allowance for room and board, but in a city like Camden, your choices were limited. Apartments required a much longer commitment time or you lost your security deposit and one month's rent. As it turned out, even living in a motel for two months wiped out most of my living allowance. My room consisted of a queen-sized bed that took up about two thirds of the room and an old TV in the corner.

I packed up my paperwork and stopped at the front desk to assign my breakfast bill to the room.

"You headed off to the colored school now?" Mrs. Naomi White, the motel manager who was appropriately named, asked.

I looked down, embarrassed for her. "Yes Ma'am. I sure am."

"You know how to get there?"

"Think so."

"Now when you get off the highway, there's a School Road that's a little rutted. That's where you need to turn. Be careful on that one."

"Okay, I will. Thanks for the heads up."

"See you at dinner."

I jumped in my old beat-up Buick and headed down the main highway (the only highway) for a good 45 minutes. And just as Mrs. White had said, School Road was just ahead. As I turned onto School Road, I smiled at the description "rutted." That sucker had craters – big craters. The road seemed to go for miles, maybe because I had to slow down to 10 mph. Ahead was the sign for Miller Academy. It was an ornate semicircular iron and brass sign attached to the fenceposts and gate. It looked more like a ranch. Beyond it were three large buildings.

A security guard stopped me at the entrance. "Can I help you?" he asked as he stepped up to my window. He was a big guy with intimidating features.

"I'm here to see Grace Fletcher."

He checked his clipboard. "Your name?"

"Alan Handler. I'm the Reading teacher."

He kept looking. "You have an appointment?"

"Yes. I'm a little early but ..."

"SALLY – " he yelled into his radio. "I got a Alan Binner here."

I tried to correct him, "That's ... Handler." He cut me off.

"You do? Well why the hell don't you people give me that information huh? Yeah ... okay ... I'll send him in."

He holstered his radio and turned back to me. "Okay, Mr. Binner just follow the road to the middle building on your left and the principal's office is right inside."

"Thank you," I offered. "Have a nice ..." He was gone.

Principal Grace Fletcher met me outside her office. She was a very pleasant bespectacled black woman in her 50s. She held out her hand and gave me a very firm handshake. "Very nice to meet you, Mr. Handler. Welcome to Miller Academy. Did you find it okay?"

"Yes I did. Thanks Mrs. Fletcher."

"May I call you Alan?"

"Of course."

"Good. Call me Grace. Hearing you call me ma'am and Mrs. Fletcher makes me feel like your mother." She looked at me closer. "Maybe even your grandmother."

Grace took me on a brief tour of the facility, including the dorms as we talked. "Now Alan, I've looked at scheduling and the best option is evening classes. I hope that's okay. These kids don't have many breaks during the day. We try to keep them busy so they don't have too much time on their hands. You'll be in Classroom 134 right here." We walked inside. "Here's your class list. There are 15 students enrolled. All need the help. Now … there are some things you need to know."I looked at the class list which were primarily girls, 11 of them, with 4 boys."These kids all have potential but they WILL test you. You're white and you're not too far from their age. You understand?"

"Oh sure. Don't you worry. I will handle it."

"You ever taught teenage black kids before?"

I thought about lying but she'd know right away.

"No ma'am … um … Grace. I haven't."

"Here's some advice. Be firm. Take control of your class right away. Try not to show fear. Got it? This building is shut down at night except for your class, so it's all you. Are you okay with that?"

"Yes." I was dying inside. I didn't have it. I was looking around knowing I was teaching at 7:30 at night in this building … the only white guy.

"Here are your keys. You start tomorrow night. Call me if you need anything."

"I will." For sure!

"Hi, Handler, I miss your face." Karol's voice was like a gift from heaven. I lay on my motel bed staring at the popcorn ceiling and the small brown circles that stained their corners.

"Miss yours, too. You doing okay?"

"Yeah. Mom's a mess though. She's losing it a little. She was singing Just a Closer Walk With Thee in the kitchen a while ago."

"I love that song."

"Me too. That's what I told her. She said she didn't know it." We both shared a laugh.

"How's your brother?"

"Kelly's so drugged up that he just stares at the wall. The place he's in is beautiful though. Got everything ... pool, tennis, lots of land. Too bad he can't really appreciate it, but I'd rather see him that way for a while than being so manic and out of control. AAHHHHH ... just want to get out of here."

"When can you come visit?"

"The doctor wants me to stay close while they adjust his meds. I think I could come after that. How's the school?"

"I'll tell you more after tomorrow night. That's when I hold my very first class."

"Are you nervous?"

"Scared shitless."

Scared Shitless could have been the title of my very own horror movie starring me and my entire class the night I pulled in to Miller Academy. It was very dark at 7p.m. and there were no lights on in the building. I unlocked the entrance and felt around for the switch, which thankfully was right next to the door. The hallways all lit up together and I could finally breathe.

As I walked down the corridor, the clicks of my heels were the only sounds in the building. I wanted to get there a little early so I could have time to get settled in the room and be there when the first students arrived. At 7:30, I was still alone. At 7:40, two girls walked in, arm-in-arm laughing, apparently about something that happened earlier.

"Good evening," I said in my professional voice.

"Hi," the shorter of the two said. "Are you our teach-a?"

"Yes," I smiled. "I'm Mr. Handler."

"We the only ones you're teachin'?" Girl number two asked.

Before I could answer, three more students came in. The first fell forward into my arms, tripped by his friends. "Sorry ..." He started to say then turned to his friend and said, "Ronnie, you are SUCH an ASSHOLE."

The three of them sat together in the last row. I looked at the clock and saw that it was already nearing 8 o'clock.

"We'll give the rest of the class a few more minutes and then start." It took about 10 more minutes before the rest of the students made their way into the room. It was chaos. A few kids were at their desks but most were still standing and talking.

"Okay ... okay. Everybody take your seats. Any seat will do." No one was really paying attention and the noise level rose higher. "HELLO! We have got to get started, ladies and gentlemen. CAN I have your attention?" No one paid an ounce of attention. I could have been part of the furniture.

I could feel the heat rise in my neck to every cell in my brain. It was the first time I could remember being this angry. Looking at the students, I honestly felt that I could shake them ... and even worse ... kill them. Every bad thing that I thought was beneath me to utter, I said in my head. I was ashamed. I was humiliated. I was scared.

Then I was just pissed off.

I grabbed the biggest book I could find from the shelf behind me. I think it was an unabridged dictionary. I stood on the desk and dropped it on the floor.

"BOOM!"

That apparently did the trick.

"SIT DOWN ..." I don't know how loud I was but certainly commanded attention. They stopped to look. Many ducked their heads before looking around. Maybe they thought it was a gun. There was momentary silence and all eyes were on me.

I very quietly said, "... Thank you."

Just then, another student slowly strolled into the room. His eyes were fixed on mine the entire time. Dressed completely in black with a black turtleneck and sunglasses and a Black Panther beret, he grabbed the last desk in the back, raised it a few inches off the ground and slammed it down for effect. He then sat down at it, still staring menacingly into my eyes.

I have to admit: I was terrified. The first hour of my very first teaching experience and I was now completely in the grips of "fight vs flight." I remembered the words of Principal Fletcher ... "Take control." How can I take control of this? I looked around. They were testing me. And I was failing miserably. The Black Panther in the back reached over and grabbed the handle of the paper cutter that was on the table adjacent to his desk. He raised it up and brought it down slowly. All the while he kept his stare on me.

I'm dying here.

I had to quickly decide what to do. I easily could have just grabbed my box of reading materials and fled. That would have been easy enough. I could quit READInc and that would be that. Or I could ...

"Okay. It seems we may have all got off on the wrong foot." I managed to say something like that. At that point, I was doing well just to get words out. My voice might have been two octaves higher for all I know. "My name is Mr. Handler," I wrote it on the board behind me. "The course I teach will help you with reading comprehension, study skills, and college prep."

"Do we have to take this class?" a skinny student with a huge afro asked.

"Well, your parents elected to have you take this course Miss ...?"

"Um ... Charleton. Berniece Charleton."

"So we gotta come here every night?" another student asked from the back.

"No, twice a week Tuesday and Thursday for six weeks." Thank God, I thought. "What's your name?"

"William."

"Hah! William? You mean Gas Man! That's what we call him." Laughter erupted at the voice from the other side of the room.

"Okay, okay. Settle down." I started to feel at least there was now a way I might get SOME control. Respect might take longer. "It's just about 8:30 and we lost a lot of time tonight. Please remember that class starts at 7:30 sharp. I'd like all of you in your seats at that time on Thursday. Let's start off fresh ... Okay? You are dismissed."

A few okays were said amid the rush of students heading out the door. I slowly sat down at my desk as they all rushed past. I stared out the window just sitting there in the silence.

It was then that I heard the sound of one more student slowly edging toward me from the back of the room. It was the Black Panther. He looked older than me as he approached and he was at least six-foot -three. He raised his fist in the air as he stopped at my desk and said, "Power to the people."

I didn't know what the appropriate response should be. I froze with my mouth open and then said, "Yes ... and I will see you Thursday, okay Mr. ...?"

And, he was gone.

"Here's what I have on your students, Alan." Principal Fletcher patted a stack of summaries sitting on her desk.

"How about the Black Panther kid?"

"You must mean Leon Washington." She thumbed through the stack until she found his and handed it to me. Exceptional IQ, big time underachiever, angry young man with lots of baggage."

"Personal problems at home?"

"His daddy is one of the most powerful criminal attorneys in Chicago and his mom sits on the city council. He's an only child."

"Wow. I thought ..."

"You thought broken home? No daddy? Lives in the projects?"

"Sorry, I guess I did."

"No need to apologize. Interestingly, Leon might have a big time case of black guilt. His tough Black Panther, street smart, kill whitey attitude might mask his true upper-crust, protected upbringing. He wants to be respected here."

I studied the folders, fascinated by the diverse backgrounds.

"They scared you last night, huh?"

"Well ... not sure scared is the right word." I looked at her face as she broke into a smile. "Yeah. Scared is the right word. Even petrified at times. I just don't know if I can make a difference. We are so different."

"We don't have many white teachers and very few your age. They need you, Alan. I know you're just here for a short time. But these are kids who can benefit from what you're showing them. I want to see them succeed and get into a college or university. You're not as different as you think."

On my bed at the motel, I spread out all the pages of information that Mrs. Fletcher gave me. I even created a cheat sheet to take to class with photos of the students and key phrases that would spark my memory. I headed to school.

Thursday night we started at 7:45. It still was not perfect but everyone was there, even Mr. Washington in his same Black Panther uniform. There were books at everyone's desk and pads and pencils that I had prearranged.

"All right, let's turn to page 32 and take eight minutes to read the story about the Space Race. I'll tell you when to start and after 10 minutes I'll ask that you close your books."

"Can we read another story instead?"

I looked at my cheat sheet. "Carla, let's stick with this one to start, okay?"

Carla looked a little shocked as I called her by name. She nodded her approval. They sat up a little straighter. "Everyone ready," I said, looking at my watch. "Begin."

I walked around the room, watching as they all seemed to be following this direction well. Even Leon seemed to be in sync. As the time drew closer. I noticed many not even close to being finished, so I gave them an extra minute and then: "Time. Close your books."

There were the moans and groans from those who hadn't finished. "It's okay – this isn't a test. But I do want to ask you about what you've read." I scanned my list.

"Jameel?" Jameel gave a quick double-take and thumbed his book nervously. "Which country was first to send a missile into outer space? USA or Soviet Union?"

"USA!" Jameel beamed.

"No. The USA was not the first."

Ten hands went up to answer the question.

"Kamela, I'm pretty sure you've got this."

"Soviet Union!" She smiled and stood up and took a bow to lots of applause.

"Okay, Kamela, so what was the name of the first Soviet satellite to orbit Earth?"

"Oh, man," she said, "I already got one answer. Ask one of these other fools."

A hand went up. "Candace?"

Candace sat removed from the others. She was shy and didn't interact with the others from what I observed. "It was S-p-u-t-n-i-k ... not sure how to say it," She answered so quietly that I could hardly hear it.

"That's correct. Sputnik. Candace ... excellent work." A big smile crept across her face.

There's hope.

The next few weeks seemed better but still not where we were making good progress. I still was not getting through to many in class. I looked out at glazed-over eyes when I talked to them about the importance of comprehension and increasing their ability to read passages quickly. I really thought the section on taking the SAT and some tips to increase their scores would have many at least interested.

Other than Candace and a couple others, they really didn't want to be there. Leon quit slicing the paper cutter and giving me the evil eye, but continued to stoically wear his Black Panther look throughout.

Things changed slightly after I happened upon a pickup basketball game on campus a few days later. Jameel had called out my name from across the way. "Mr. Handler … wanna play? We're short a guy."

There are those times in life when you make a decision that you know in your heart of hearts is a good decision to make but will probably also be one you regret for years to come. Playing pick-up ball with a group of kids who are in top shape and play every day together and look down on you (literally) because they average a height differential of five inches … well, let's just say it's somewhat intimidating. Your mind is screaming at you to just keep walking but you know you have to do this … to prove yourself … to gain respect.

Even if it kills you.

"Kills" is the operative word. Street ballers have their own code. There are no fouls called unless you do it yourself, and forever be seen as weak and unable to take care of yourself. Of course, no one does it.

The game didn't go well for me. I spent the majority of the time on my butt, bloody knees and elbows, absorbing blows from the opposition as they deftly whizzed by me on the way to scoring baskets at will. I actually made one or two shots myself … all from outside … as I don't think I came within a few feet dribbling to the basket.

Somewhere close to the end of the game, I think they all felt concerned that I literally might not make it out alive. I was laid out on the brink of unconsciousness after a particularly brutal elbow to the jaw from an opposing player. Jameel knelt next to me, "You okay Mr. Handler? Let me help you."

Jameel reached out his hand, but I bravely (stupidly) brushed off his hand and got to my feet. "Thanks, but I got this, Jameel. I'm staying in." I wobbled on my feet but stood upright and did in fact finish the game.

My entire body ached when I finally made it back to the motel. Getting out of my car was actually an out-of-body experience. I watched myself in slow motion trying to put one foot in front of another. I was bruised and scraped and bloodied, but managed to find my room and my room key. The only thing keeping me upright was the thought of soon collapsing in my own bed … so close.

I turned the key and pushed open the door and – what's this? Someone's sleeping in MY bed! The Goldilocks reference couldn't be missed. My very own Goldilocks was asleep in my bed: Karol Rae Ballard, herself! I didn't want to disturb her, so I gently crawled into bed next to her and passed out cold.

When I awoke, I was alone again.

"Karol?" I looked around from my prone position and I was indeed alone. Maybe I had dreamed that she was there to begin with. I certainly didn't dream up my injuries. Each turn in the bed was a painful reminder of how shitty I had played on the court. I pushed up on the bed, groaning as I propped up my pillows, and there on my lap was a note and an envelope.

"Dear Bloody Mess, I drove to the pharmacy to get something for your war wounds. I'm so depressed that you decided to engage in knife fights and didn't invite me to participate. I'll pick up a pizza on my way back. Check out the letter from READInc. Good news. Kisses, K."

Goldilocks was here after all. The envelope was already opened. It was actually addressed to both of us. Inside was the formal notification of our next assignment. We were going together to Indiana. Karol was to teach at an all-girls' school in South Bend and I was assigned to a boarding school in LaPorte just 25 miles away. Both schools looked beautiful in pictures and were excellent academically from what I read in the paperwork that was sent. We would start in three weeks. Miller Academy was done in two. Perfect!

"Let's celebrate, Scabby!" Karol came up behind me and kissed my neck. I turned and threw her onto the bed. "Take off your clothes," she said forcefully. Who was I to resist? I practically ripped them off and she pushed me onto the bed.

"First things first!" She took out a big wad of cotton and hydrogen peroxide.

"Hurt me honey."

She did.

Afterward we sat crosslegged in the bed, naked, eating the most delicious pizza I ever tasted. It was probably just cheese on a piece of cardboard but it was heaven sitting across from Karol, and even the crummy little room seemed wonderful with her in it.

"So ... here's what I thought. I'll stay here for a week and then drive to South Bend to look for an apartment, and you can meet me there when you finish. I figure South Bend being a college town has lots more apartments than LaPorte. Right?"

"You would think."

Karol opened her bag and took out a perfectly rolled joint. "Shall we?"

"Why not?" I said as I took her lighter and fired it up. I had a brief case of paranoia when I thought about the rednecks who run this place, but felt comforted with the knowledge that they had never once come by when I was there. I took a long, wonderful pull and floated to the ceiling. It had been so long.

"So how are your little criminals here?"

My high came crashing down. "Not great, K. I think they hate me."

"That why they beat the shit out of you?" She pointed to my bruises.

"Yeah, a friendly basketball game."

"I didn't know you played."

"I watched most of it from the prone position."

She laughed. "Seriously, did you make any progress with them? You've gotta do a post test, remember."

"Don't remind me. I have no idea how they are gonna do." I took another hit after Karol passed the joint. "You know, funny thing. Well, I don't know if it's funny ... but when I first saw them and they paid no attention and were so rude, I hated them. Really. I am embarrassed to say that I was just like every racist redneck in this place. I looked at them as stupid and shiftless and I was ashamed of myself." I reached over and grabbed an open beer from the night before.

"But over time, I really have grown kinda attached to them. There's a sweet girl named Candace who's a loner but smart as a whip, a skinny kid named Jameel who has potential and this Black Panther dude named Leon who tries too hard to be the cool, white-people slayer."

"Lovely."

I realized how crazy it must sound to Karol. "Oh well. Tomorrow's another day and soon we will be in Indiana and this will all be a distant memory."

I was feeling pretty happy when I walked into my classroom. Maybe it was the thought of Karol lying in my bed or maybe it was the two hits I took from the remnants of Karol's joint in my ashtray. Either way, it started as a good night. Candace met me at the door and handed me an envelope. She never made eye contact and hurried to her desk. I opened the envelope and pulled an elaborate invitation for the Miller Academy Senior Class Prom. It was adorned with stars that spelled out "A Night Under The Stars." I looked over at Candace, who glanced at me with her head down and I smiled and mouthed "thank you." It was the first time I actually saw her shy grin become a real smile.

I looked at the rest of the class and was amazed that most of them were patiently sitting in their seats. Other than Candace, who had her book ready and was ready to read, most of the others had headsets on listening to music, or passing notes to each other. They were patient, but they were bored out of their minds.

"You know, I was just thinking," I said to the group, "I'm here looking at your faces and wondering, if you are enjoying this at all? I mean ... really ... do you care about any of this shit?" That got their attention. Eyes opened wider. A few heads came together giggling. "Yeah, I said shit. I know it's not politically correct for your teacher to say it but sometimes it's the perfect descriptor to use."

Jameel raised his hand. "Yo, Mr. Handler. I got a question ... How about you? Do you care about any of this shit?"

I started laughing. "The politically correct response would be ... 'of course I care. This course is designed to be blah blah blah ...' Truth is, this stuff can be tedious and boring at times. It's not meant to be fun. Most of the time it's probably not but it's a means to an end. These are exercises that are meant to give you the skills to use later in college. So I guess I'd say ... (I picked up a book) ... I don't REALLY care a lot about this shit. But I DO care about you."

All eyes were now fixed on my words. "Hey, I got an idea. Tonight I want you to think really hard about this. I want you to write this out for me ... Where do you see yourself after graduation? I mean ... what is it you want to achieve? Are you going back home? Working? Career? Married? College? Don't worry about making this into a composition just random thoughts are fine. I know some of it might not even be on your radar ... But think about it."

For the next 30 minutes, everyone in that classroom was furiously writing.

It was a good night.

The next evening, Karol and I sat down to dinner in the motel dining room. I had brought along the papers that my students worked on and really wanted to share them. It was All You Can Eat Shrimp Night at the Camden Motel and a treat that apparently is a "must have" based on the size of the crowd. It happened only on the first Friday of the month and we jammed our little selves into a corner booth. I was amazed at the size of the crowd (and the size of the customers as well). Plates overflowing with shrimp and fries flew out of the kitchen and were immediately scarfed up by the hungry crowd.

Karol looked around the room and said, "Hey. Check out couple number one, three tables to the right."

He had on a plaid sports coat with a chocolate brown nylon shirt and kind of yellowish pants. He topped the scales at about 290 and his spouse was close behind. White framed winged glasses and a colorful scarf over her hair. Sleeveless denim blouse (God help us), tight white pants and sandals rounded it out.

"Okay. Here goes," I said. "I'm gonna guess that his name is Henry and he's the Youth Minister at First United Methodist. Her name is Marge and she is the secretary for a local construction company that her daddy owns."

Karol cleared her throat and began the conversation as Marge matching her words to Marge's lip movements, "I do declare, Henry, this shrimp is so much better than last month's."

Me (as Henry), "Yes. I agree. Seems like last time the shrimp was smaller and not nearly as tasty."

Karol, "Well if you ask me ... I think Jimmy, the cook was fiddling with the new waitress in the back last month instead of keeping an eye on cooking the shrimp. She's not here tonight!"

Me, "Now Marge. Not very Christian of you to say that."

Karol, "Oh stick it up your ass, Henry."

I almost coughed up my last shrimp with that comment. Our friends Henry and Marge looked over surprised.

"Okay, okay." I was still choking on a shrimp but managed to catch my breath and point to our next couple. "Check out Elvis Presley's cousin Earl in the far corner." The guy had the Elvis' slicked back hair and orange suspenders holding up his khakis.

"Earl brought his girlfriend Ruby to dine." Karol added. "Ruby" had teased blonde hair with multiple clips holding on for dear life. Polyester pink pantsuit was her clothing of choice.

Me (as Earl): "Ruby, you gonna finish those fries?"

Karol (as Ruby): "Yes I am, Earl. Why don't you just order some more? It's all you can eat, silly."

"Duh! I am so stupid. Of course."

"Earl ... while you're at it, tell the waitress to bring more ketchup."

"I can't remember ... is that part of the same all-you-can eat special?"

Karol gave me a high five and laughed a loud, manly laugh that was so distinctive. It made me laugh, as well. Even when the jokes were not that funny, that laugh could make the whole room crack up.

When we finished dessert, and the waitress cleared our plates, I pulled out my briefcase and took out the papers. "Are those the papers that your students filled out yesterday about what their goals were?"

I handed them to her. "Yeah. Tell me what you think."

Karol read them one by one as we sat there. "Wait till you see what Jameel said."

"Shhhhh." She waved a finger at me. "Let me read them all."

I noticed that as she finished each one she separated them into piles. Sometimes she would fold a corner or change her mind and move a pile. God, she was beautiful, sitting there reading. Her glasses sat on the tip of her nose so precariously that it seemed like the slightest movement or sneeze would have flung them across the table. "Okay, I've got some questions."

"Shoot," I countered.

"Leon." Karol grabbed the first sheet in the first pile. "Interesting statements he makes about fighting for freedom, special training in the militia and then switches gears and says he wants to be a defense attorney."

"He's my Huey Newton ... Black Panther. Little bit of an identity crisis because he comes from money but doesn't want to admit it publicly."

"I see. Seems like a bright kid, huh?"

"I think so. Doesn't speak in class and I think he wants to kill me with a paper cutter."

"I'd like to kill you with a paper cutter sometimes, too," she said, smiling."Um ... Candace is the complete opposite." Karol held up Candace's paper. "She has a crush on you. Look at all these hearts and smiley faces."

"Okay, okay," I waved my hands. "I have one crush and 14 death threats."

"Not true. There's a lot of good stuff in these papers." Karol picked up a stack of papers. "There are about a half dozen of these kids that really seem to care, Alan. If I were you, I'd try to meet with each of these kids one on one. You know?"

I thought for a moment about the brilliance of this idea. The names that Karol chose were the leaders in class. Since I probably didn't have time to meet with everybody in class, meeting with this select group who at least showed interest would be the next best thing. And their influence on others (if I could influence them more) would be just what I needed to give the rest a boost.

"You're so smart. That's why I keep you around."

"I know," she said with a wicked smile. "Let's go back to the room. I just bought a new paper cutter I wanted to try out."

Karol's idea worked like a charm. I had worked out a plan that could be implemented within the next week and would not affect the students' class schedules.

I started with Leon. He would be the toughest and the one that I felt if I could break through even a little would be a huge win and make the rest of my meetings so much easier. So, I took him to play Putt Putt golf. After about 30 minutes of Leon coming up with numerous excuses why he couldn't go and wouldn't be comfortable he finally admitted that he had never played before and that he thought that it was a dorky game. He also said he would be humiliated if anyone from school saw him.

"Sure it's a dorky game," I said. "Do you really think anyone from school would be there? That's why I picked it."

That's all he needed to hear and we were off. Trying to look cool while you're hitting a tiny ball into Dumbo's trunk is impossible. Leon had to shed all of the Black Panther pretense and we ultimately had a good conversation. He shared some very personal information about his family. Dad was a top attorney in Chicago who had built an incredible reputation. He was tough on Leon, who was both so proud of his dad and at the same time ashamed of the defense of some of his more questionable clients. Leon's dad represented gangsters, accused murderers and high profile white collar criminals. He also did a great deal of pro bono work in the community.

Leon's mom was not the average stay-at-home housewife. She served on the city council for many years after a successful career in real estate. She also raised three children. Leon's older brother Eric was an attorney in Dad's firm and his sister was married to a banker with a family of her own in Cincinnati. Leon was the baby by 10 years. He was the product of a series of boarding schools that his father insisted on to give him some structure and some independence.

Leon felt completely alone. He felt a sense of unworthiness. His mom and dad and his brother and sister had achieved so much. He felt he would never be able to reach what his family had achieved. That's why, of course, he created this new identity as a Black Panther as a cover for his insecurities.

"You know, Leon, I don't think you give yourself enough credit," I said to him after I hit Dumbo in the right eye with my next shot.

"I don't?"

"Well for one thing, you beat the hell out of me at putt putt golf".

"Yeah but Mr. Handler, you're pretty shitty at this game."

We both shared a laugh. I then stood next to him and said, "Most people think that growing up with money would give you an incredible advantage. They don't see the pressures of coming from a family with great expectation. Sometimes it's easier to have a family that you don't feel so pressured to be exceptional. You, my friend, have exceptional talents that I'm sure you have yet to realize. You're a smart kid, Leon. I noticed on your paper that you turned in, you want to be a defense attorney just like your dad."

"Not just like my dad. I want to defend people who he doesn't defend ... people without money and who don't have a voice."

"I know I'm just an old white guy. But I'd love to help you if you'd let me."

Leon looked at me for a long time and then said, "Only if you could help me better than you can play putt putt."

"That I can do."

Jameel and I went for burgers after class one night. It was a greasy burger joint just a few blocks from campus. He ate like a starving man. After the third hamburger, I lost count. Jameel and I already had a pretty good rapport, so talking about personal family life was not that difficult. He grew up in New Jersey. His mother had been married twice and was currently divorced. He was living with his grandmother because his mother was unemployed and unable to care for him. Neither of his dads were in the picture. Jameel had a little sister who was five years old and the way he talked about her brought a tear to my eye. She was the love of his life and he cared for her deeply. Jameel was on scholarship.

He had written in his essay that he didn't want to go to college and I wondered why. His loves were pretty focused on basketball and his little sister and his outside interests were limited. "So why not college?" I asked.

"Nothing against college, Mr. Handler I just don't think I'd be very good at it."

"Is it college in general or just certain colleges?" I asked.

"I guess it's colleges in general. I really don't know much about colleges that are out there."

"If you and I took a visit to USC right down the road in Columbia, would you like to see that campus?"

"Sure. But I don't want to waste your time, Mr. Handler. I'm not sure I could get in, anyway."

"Just let me worry about that."

Over my right shoulder was a silhouette of someone walking up to our table. I could tell by the look in Jameel's eyes that this silhouette was not a friendly one. His look was both frightened and angry. "Well lookee here," the stranger said. "You guys are just sitting here having a hamburger. Ain't that cute?" The massive red-faced intruder looked to be in his forties and smelled like a brewery. I looked over at his table and saw four more large white men with blank expressions staring at us, with food coming out of their mouths. "Is that your nigger?"

Jameel put his hands on the arms of the chair to stand and I grabbed him before he did. "You know that was an unkind word that you called my friend here." I said.

"Oh, the nigger's your friend? How sweet are you on him? Are you guys dating?" I pushed my seat back then and stood nose-to-nose. Realizing that I might be close to death didn't seem to matter then, as my temper had risen.

As luck would have it, Karol happened to walk through the door. She was going to order a hamburger for herself when she spotted us and scooted right over to our table. She happened to hear that last sentence. "Why, honey," Karol said to me, "I thought you were sweet on ME. I had no idea."

The redneck looked at Karol and said, "Hey there, little lady. Don't worry about this loser. if you're looking for a real man you just look in this direction."

Karol stepped back and looked at him and said, "The only thing I see in your direction is a big old fat redneck who is rude and crude and has little hands. Do you know what that means?"

Stupidly, he looked at his hands with a puzzled look as Karol escorted him over to his table and told his buddies, "Can you boys explain what I said to Bluto here?" She turned to leave and then stopped and looked over her shoulder. " By the way, I've already talked to the manager and he's over there on the phone ready to make a call for me if we have any more trouble. Night, boys."

Karol sat in the chair that I pulled out for her. I introduced her to Jameel, who just belted out. "Wow … you the most awesome white lady I ever met. Mr. Handler, you are a lucky man."

"I like this guy!" Karol gave Jameel a great big hug.

I took the three other kids together. They were all female and of course one of them was Candace, who already was a wonderful student and totally engaged. I took the three of them on a picnic in one of the beautiful Camden parks and we had a great discussion about life after high school. Candace wanted to be a veterinarian and had already done her research as to how she needed to get that done. She had a great love for animals and wanted to dedicate her life to help. Haley wanted to be in public relations. She wasn't exactly sure what that meant; so we had a good discussion about what that job really does. Afterwards, I think, she was even more excited to get into the field. Jasmine wanted to be a fashion designer. She loved clothes and designed outfits for all of her friends.

I felt I was finally making some progress. The five students that I had meetings with seemed to generate much more interest and excitement in where we were going. I really thought Karol's idea had merit and that perhaps these meetings might have that viral good feeling effect I had hoped for.

After dropping off the three girls, I hurried back to the motel to tell Karol about my progress. When I opened the door, my heart sank. Her suitcases were gone and there was a note on the bed. I picked it up and read:

> "Alan ... my brother is worse. Heading home to check on the family and then driving to Indiana to find us a place to live. I'll call you with the information. Karol."

Nothing personal. No "sorry I didn't stay to say goodbye" or "I'll be thinking about you" or God forbid "love you." That was Karol. I should've been used to it by now. She would just appear and then disappear over and over. If I were a psychiatrist, I would say that she had attachment issues. But, in truth, I really wasn't sure whether it was a personality issue or she just really wasn't committed to our relationship or maybe the dreaded, "She's really not into me."

Actually, I wasn't sure what our relationship was. Some might say it wasn't even a relationship. It was convenient for us to travel together as a couple and we obviously had affection for each other. She was just the kind of girl that was easy to get attached to and I was hooked. Besides, the plan was what we had discussed before: She had always intended to leave before the end of my program to travel to Indiana to find us a place to live.

The next two weeks were so much better than the first four. The students all seemed to be making progress and I finally felt a sense of accomplishment. I actually enjoyed going to class and seeing them and I really felt a sense of sadness as the days counted down to the end of the program. Leon didn't wear the beret anymore and stopped playing with the paper cutter, Jameel sat straight in his desk ... kind of ... and, of course, the girls still giggled but participated fully in class readings.

The senior prom was held a few days before the course ended. I was actually very impressed with how the students transformed the drab gymnasium. Stars were everywhere, covered with glitter, accented with spotlights and a huge banner announced A NIGHT UNDER THE STARS hung over the covered stage.

Principal Fletcher greeted me when I entered. "So, Mr. Handler, I know that your time is coming to an end here at Miller Academy."

"That it is, Mrs. Fletcher."

"And you survived, I see."

I smiled and glanced at the crowd of snappily dressed

students in all their colorful dresses and smart tuxes. "I did. Actually, I thoroughly enjoyed myself these last few weeks and will miss everyone I've met."

Principal Fletcher eyed a group of students heading toward us. "I believe you made some new friends."

The students surrounded us as Candace stepped in front holding a present wrapped in colorful paper with glittering stars. "Mr. Handler, we um, just wanted to tell you how much we appreciate you and how great it was to have you as our teacher." Candace handed me the present.

"I am overwhelmed. You have taught me more than I have taught you. I know you all will do great things and I look forward to hearing about them in the future." We hugged and then they escorted me to the dance floor. Mrs. Fletcher laughed as I tried to do my white dance moves in the middle of a very cool dance line of students.

I left exhausted later in the night. Sitting there in my car, I thought about how special this place really was. I opened the present that the students gave me and felt the emotions getting even stronger. It was the record album soundtrack from To Sir With Love, the movie starring Sidney Poitier about a black teacher who won over the affections of white students in the classroom.

I cried my eyes out.

CHAPTER THREE

Indiana Wants Me

I knew that the trip to South Bend would take me at least two days. It was a good twelve hours from Camden and my old '69 Buick was not the most reliable vehicle on the road.

I loaded all my stuff on Friday and pulled into Miller Academy for one last goodbye before heading off. Saying goodbye to the students at Miller was tougher than I thought. I was really going to miss those guys. I left feeling proud. Their improvement scores on the post test brought rave reviews from the team in New Orleans, who were very generous in their compliments.

Karol was proud of me too.

She called me the day before to build up my fragile ego. She also shared her nervousness about beginning her new career in Indiana as a first-time teacher and how much my determination had inspired her. Funny, I had never seen that side of her. She had always seemed so fearless to me.

Tentatively, she gave me the directions to our new "home," which was located outside of South Bend, Indiana: a mobile home park. "Really?" I had asked her.

"Yes," she said. "That's right. A mobile home park, a big one with lots of double wides, furnished and ready to occupy. And one has our name on it." Karol apparently searched for days and couldn't find apartments or affordable rentals that would let us live there for less than six months without forfeiting security deposits. "Besides", she said, "The double wides are very cute and the park is clean."

Armed with the information I needed and unfolding multiple maps of all the states I would drive through, I headed through the Carolina mountains and slipped in a tape mix of travel music from James Taylor and John Denver to Randy Newman. It was a perfect set for the mountains.

As I passed through Asheville, North Carolina, I remembered the summer trips we used to take when I was a young boy before Dad got sick. There was a ranch outside Hendersonville that seemed like it was as big as a city. Gary and I used to ride the horses for miles and spend our nights by a huge campfire roasting marshmallows and telling lies.

Gary was four years older than me. He was the family favorite. When he was born, he had golden blond hair and a perfect smile. Nobody else in the family had that color hair. The rest of us were dark. When he came along, it was like he was the prince … in fact my mom called him that often. I don't think they had a nickname for me back then, unless it was shithead or something like that.

Gary and I were very close.

He took care of me back then when we were growing up. And I remember when we visited the ranch, I tagged along with him everywhere and hung on his every word.

After Dad died of lung cancer we never went back to the ranch again.

Just about the time that Randy Newman was finishing *Mama Told Me Not To Come* ("Will you have whiskey with your water /Or sugar with your tea"), I pulled into the Sunset Motel in Lexington, Kentucky. It was just about halfway to my final destination and a perfect point to stop and get some rest. It just so happened that it was also the home of Red State BBQ. The gas station attendant was the one who recommended it. He told me, "Don't be fooled when you pull up. It's ugly as sin and the place looks like it's about to fall down but the barbecue is the best you ever had."

He was right.

The ribs were big and tender and the sauce was to die for. It was spicy and sweet and the flavor stayed on your tongue for a few minutes longer after you put it in your mouth. Most people say that barbecue places are all alike. Those are the people who don't eat barbecue a lot. The places like Red State have been around for decades, not years, and the smell of the food is infused in the walls and the floors ... even the distinct sounds of the servers and the customers have a certain rhythm. There were only six tables in the whole restaurant and there was one server who was taking care of everyone in the place. When I finished I was perfectly satisfied.

The motel was a different story. It was old, it was small and it was a fairly scary place. I was so tired I didn't really mind. Just there for a couple hours to rest my head. When I walked into the front lobby (a broom closet with a desk) I asked for the second floor. The folks congregating in front of the first floor rooms looked a little sketchy. The clerk was very accommodating, "Suit yourself. Not sure all them rooms on the second floor have been cleaned as well."

He also was right.

I was too tired to switch rooms or complain. I had a blanket in my car and an extra pillow that I always carried with me because it might come in handy. Well ... okay ... it was soft and I had it as a kid. So what?

I slept a little longer than planned. Between the ribs and the beer the night before, I had fallen asleep fully dressed with my shoes still on. But by 10:00, I was well on my way to Indiana. This half of the trip called for a new tape mix. Jerry Lee Lewis, Kinky Friedman, Stones and a touch of Ernie K-Doe should do it. I needed the funk and the big sounds to keep me awake. I had a little Freddie Mercury in reserve if needed.

When I got to Cincinnati, I pulled into an Esso station to get gas. I asked the attendant where Izzy's Deli was located. A college buddy, Steve Greenbaum, was from Cincy and told me if I was ever in the general vicinity to try Izzy's, the best deli in the world.

Of course, he was right.

The sounds and smells of Izzy's brought back such wonderful memories of my Aunt Jeanette cooking in our kitchen. Just as Red State BBQ the day before infused my senses with its rich, distinctive aroma so had Izzy's as soon as I opened the door. I couldn't wait to dive into a big fat juicy corned beef sandwich, a huge pickle and a bowl of matzoh ball soup.

Heaven.

When I jumped back in the car, totally satisfied and stomach full with Jewish comfort food. I was now on the back stretch, only a few hours from South Bend. I cranked on the radio and played *They Ain't Makin Jews Like Jesus Anymore* by Kinky Friedman, his totally irreverent farce about a Jewish guy and a redneck in a barroom brawl: "We don't turn the other cheek, the way we done before."

By the time I reached Indianapolis it was mid afternoon.

This was my uncle's hometown. My dad's brother managed a pretty large pawn shop downtown Indy. Uncle Benny was a sweet old guy with a temperament that hardly matched his profession. I could never imagine him haggling with a customer over price or value much less dealing with the type of characters that come in and out all day long. His wife, however, my Aunt Jeanette, was completely the opposite. She was tough as nails and hated just about everyone she dealt with. Maybe Uncle Benny worked the back of the shop and she took care of the front.

I thought about stopping at the shop but didn't want to get to South Bend too late. I would be only a couple of hours from Indianapolis for the next eight weeks so I could easily come back to visit.

I really never got to see them much. My mom didn't care for Jeanette's grating personality. But, I remember when my dad was at his sickest and not expected to live another year, Jeanette flew to New Orleans and cooked for us for a week. She and Uncle Benny stayed in our room while Gary and I slept in the living room. She was a great cook, especially with Jewish comfort food like brisket and potato latkes and matzoh ball soup. Mom hated cooking. We lived on sandwiches and scrambled eggs. She used the oven for storage.

When my dad, Morris Handler, died at 42 years old, my mom Sylvia went into deep depression. My grandmother, my mother's mother, moved in and really took over the household for the next two years. I really loved my grandmother. In later years, she and I drank beer together on the front porch.

Grandma Ruthie told great stories about my Grampa Max. I never got to know him because he died when I was two. But through my Grandma Ruthie's eyes, he was a giant of a man.

"Oh, Allie (only she called me that) ... your grandfather was such a great man. Six-foot-five and strong as an ox, he was. Every day when he'd come home from working on the docks, he would stop and get me fresh flowers, even when we couldn't afford to buy dinner. He'd still get me flowers. Who knows? Maybe he picked them out of somebody's garden, but he would always bring them home. Can you imagine? Here he was all day long, moving big old crates and lifting hundreds of pounds, breaking his back, but he still was so sweet."

Gary told me once that Grandpa Max was really about five-foot-ten and worked in the shipping office of a steamship company. Gary always seemed to find out things that I never knew. I guess that comes with being the big brother. Funny, I always believed Gary above anyone else. Even when he might be telling me some tall story. I didn't care. His word was the gospel. I guess that comes with being the younger brother.

As I got closer, thoughts of Karol popped into my mind. I still had lots of questions like "Why had she left me a note instead of talking to me before she left Camden?" And: "Why had she not called me since she'd been gone until the day before I left to give me directions?" I knew that she cared about me – us – but she was an enigma at times. Karol was a free spirit. I know that the tighter I held on, the more she would feel suffocated and the quicker she would want to bolt.

Ernie K-Doe sang *A Certain Girl* just as I pulled into the mobile home park via Karol's directions: "There's a Certain

Girl I've been in Love with A long Long Time / What's her name? / Can't tell you / Nooo." I smiled as I sang the lyrics. I smiled even more broadly as I found our new double wide. There were a dozen arrows stuck in the ground pointing at the front door. On the door was a big sign with multi colored letters that read: This Is Alan and Karol's New Home!!!

"There's a certain girl … "

I got up early but I didn't get out of bed. I just lay there with my head propped up on my arm looking at Karol sleep. I know how cheesy that sounds and I even felt cheesier doing it. She truly was one of the most beautiful creatures I had ever seen. Her skin was almost transparent it was so white and flawless. Her blonde hair fell in a way that framed her face and made her look even more angelic. One eye opened slowly and looked at me.

"Handler. Are you staring at me?"

I quickly looked around the room. "No."

"Yes you were. Go back to sleep."

At least it wasn't "What the fuck are you doing?" (although I heard it come out a little like that).

I looked at the ashtray filled with cigarettes and a few half burned joints. There were beer bottles and open bags of pretzels and chips strewn on the coffee table. The night before was a homecoming to remember.

"Okay, I'm up." Karol said as she tousled my hair playfully. She gave me a big kiss on the mouth and hopped out of bed to the bathroom.

Our new place was actually very comfortable. Double-wide is really a misnomer that's confusing even to owners of these manufactured homes. The real description should be "double longs" because they consist of two actual segments that are attached end to end to make a long rectangular structure. They are located in Mobile Home Parks but aren't even mobile because they are anchored to the ground and not moved. So in effect we had a double-long, non-mobile home … just like the neighbors. It reminded me a little of the structure of shotgun houses in New Orleans. Same principle of a long, narrow house that got its name from the old saying "you can shoot a shotgun from the front door and right through the back door." The furnishings were simple and fairly new. Karol did good.

"Hungry?" Karol asked as she came out of the bathroom.

"Always," I said. "What do we have?"

"Nothing. Sorry, I didn't go grocery shopping yesterday, but there's a great little diner right down the street."

"I'll drive," I said.

My old Buick was choking as I cranked the ignition. "That doesn't sound too good," Karol said.

"I know. Been this way for the last half of the drive."

Karol frowned. "Better get it checked out. Lots of miles back and forth to La Porte." I nodded and felt the car vibrating as we pulled away. "I drove by your school. It's beautiful. Looks like a college campus with the dorms and classrooms surrounded by big old oak trees."

"That's cool."

FOR THOSE WHO CAN

Karol took out her sunglasses from her purse and a bag of grass fell on the floor by her feet.

"Whoa! Did that spill over?"

"No. Thank God. I forgot I had this in my purse." She reached for the glove compartment. "Mind if I put this in here? I don't want to carry it around when we go to the diner."

"Sure. That was pretty strong stuff last night."

"I know. Right?" She closed the compartment. "I figure we've got a few more days of semi vacation before we start teaching and ..."

"Wait. Do you smell that?" I put the car in park. Something wasn't right. I heard a swooshing sound and smelled something close to burning rubber. I looked under the dash and there was a dripping liquid flame coming down onto the floorboard. That was the swoosh ... "Karol, get out of the car!" We both jumped out and stood on the sidewalk. I was looking from side to side. "I need to get something to put this out or maybe I should look under the hood."

Then it happened.

The car lit up in flames right where we were sitting just minutes before. "Oh shit. I can't believe it." Karol grabbed my arm and pulled me back to a safer distance. By now, neighbors were standing on their porches and calling out to one another. "Call the Fire Department!" There was an older man standing next to me. "That yours, son?"

I shakily said "Yeah."

"Great car, those Buicks. Mine been running fine for 20 years. But ya gotta take care of 'em you know?"

Just as I was about to say something really intelligent like "Oh yeah", the car burst into larger flames, which now took over the entire inside. I looked at Karol and she looked at me. "Did you have anything valuable in the trunk or on the seats?"

"No, thank God," I said. "I unloaded all my clothes and stuff last night. There's some paperwork in the glove compartment and ..."

"Oh shit." Karol said as we watched the fire grow stronger.

"The glove compartment has to be totally burned up by now." I said. "Nothing can survive that." That's when the fire hit the gas tank and an explosion rocked us where we stood.

The fire trucks arrived at the same time. They were surrounding the car with tanks and hoses and foam. The chief came up to me asking questions about the car and contents. "Is there anything in the car that can be explosive?"

Too late for that, I thought. "No sir."

"Are you folks alright? Do we need an ambulance?" He looked us over.

"We got out in time, thanks."

One of the firemen called to the chief. "Bill, come over here for a minute. Found something."

I saw the two men huddling around an object and then looking over at us with questioning faces. That's when the realization hit me.

The chief walked over. "This was in the glove compartment son." He held out the plastic baggie filled with an ounce of marijuana that was slightly singed in the corners but barely touched by the roaring fire. I looked at Karol, whose eyes were like saucers.

"I ... um ... I think ..." The words just didn't come.

"You need to wait here with these gentlemen while we straighten this out." Two firemen took me to the curb and stood in as the volunteer security guards.

Karol was gone.

I felt totally paralyzed. Sitting there looking at my charred, discolored car in shambles as firemen ripped the interiors out and waiting for the chief to come back to do … what? Am I being reported? Does he give me a warning? I didn't have to wait long for my answer. Two policeman pulled up and spent a few minutes talking to the fire chief. They turned and walked in my direction and asked me to stand.

"Sir, you know that more than 30 grams of marijuana was found in your glove compartment by Chief Williams?"

"Um … yes, he showed me it. But I don't know who put it there."

"Before we go any further I must tell you that you have a right to an attorney …" As he read me my rights I felt like I was in some movie … a horror movie. I couldn't breathe. I felt like I was going to drop to my knees when he put my hands behind my back and put handcuffs on. He and his partner helped me into the back seat of his cruiser and we were gone. My car was a fading sight and Karol was nowhere to be seen.

Turned out that Indiana had the strictest marijuana possession laws of any state in the union. Possession of more than 30 grams of marijuana was considered a felony. I was given all this information when we arrived at the police station for my initial booking procedures. Fingerprints, mug shots, lots of sitting and waiting in multiple rooms while the officers had donuts and coffee and got a big laugh at the fact that the weed they now held went through a major fire unscathed.

I'm not sure how long I was there, but another policeman handcuffed me again and took me to his police van waiting outside. "Where are you taking me?"

"Michigan City. Time for the big boys."

Michigan City was just outside of La Porte and about a 45-minute drive. It was the home of Indiana State Penitentiary. It was a federal prison and one of the most famous in history. John Dillinger was a prisoner there as were many on the most wanted list.

And me.

I was just about to be incarcerated as a felon. A felon! All I could think about was Arlo Guthrie and Alice's Restaurant. It's the story about Arlo getting arrested for littering and getting thrown into prison with murderers and rapists and telling them what he was in for. I imagined, just like Arlo, sitting in prison with rapists and murderers and deviants and them asking me "What are you in for?" And I would have to sheepishly tell them The Ballad of The Burning Car and an Ounce of Grass.

When we pulled up to the facility, I think my heart literally stopped. It was massive. The big steel doors opened to let the van through and I saw at least a dozen guards standing in towers at the top of the massive wall. There was another gate and I think a third as well before we came to a stop outside of the entrance itself. I was led to a series of doors that led to the area where I dropped off everything like wallet, money, keys, belt, including my shoes, into a big envelope. I was then again fingerprinted. This time there were multiple sheets that I was told to press my fingers and hands. Stupidly I said, "Oh, I did this already at the other prison."

"Boy ... this is Federal. We do our own. PRESS." The lovely female prison guard explained so that even I could understand. The same process for mug shots taken numerous times. I guess when you are in the big boy prison, they really want to get to know you well.

I was then put in a holding area with about 30 other deviants all either waiting to go to their permanent cells or maybe spending the night. I had no idea. Two of them were shackled on their legs and arms and were holding mattresses. I don't think they were in there for littering or even smoking a joint or two. I tried to make myself invisible and blend into the wall but I think they still saw me. The room was lined with concrete benches along the walls and there was a toilet toward the back but out in the open. No partition. And there was a big, fat, ugly guy sitting there doing his business as he stared down anyone who watched.

I was there for over two hours. I made one friend. The guy sitting next to me had a series of really badly drawn tattoos on his arms and around his neck. They were so bad that I couldn't even figure out what they were supposed to be. One looked like a dachshund with a suitcase ... which I figured out later was supposed to be a penis. He had a few sayings like "live 4 today" but the 4 was backwards. Maybe it was supposed to be. There was a picture of his mother on his neck that might have been his girlfriend. Oh well. He was the only one that really talked. "You from around here, buddy?" he asked me.

"No. Just moved here." Oh God. Don't ask me what I was arrested for. Please. I don't want everyone to hear it.

"I'm Smitty," he said and held out his hand.

Whew. "Handler," I said as I shook it.

"Your first time?"

"Yeah," Oh shit, here it comes.

"My fifth," he said. "They'll put me back in my old cell block I guess. I don't mind. Ain't got shit out there, you know?

Here I get fed and get what I need and I get away from my old lady for a while."

"What about your job?"

He laughed out loud as did at least a dozen others who heard my stupid question. "I think I can wash dishes at another bar when I get out. Not like I'm on the executive search list."

The cell door opened and one of the two guards looked at his clipboard. "Handler, Alan!"

I stood immediately. "Yes sir. That's me."

"Come with me, Handler."

Smitty wished me well and I did the same. The guard took me down the long hallway to another door to an empty cell with a cot. "You gonna spend the night here."

I looked around and breathed a sigh of relief. One cot, so I guess I'll be solo. "Thanks." The door closed and the guard locked me in.

The silence was deafening.

The muscles in my neck had stiffened up overnight. When I sat up in my cot, I couldn't turn my head in either direction. I tried some light stretching, which relieved it slightly but the tension kept it pretty locked up. There was a tray of food on the bench next to my cot. I assumed it was probably breakfast because I had sent back dinner. I told the guard I wasn't really hungry but the truth is that I lost my appetite when I looked at the mystery meat and bluish colored boiled potatoes. I hoped that this morning's breakfast was a little more appetizing.

Before I got a chance to check it out, a guard unlocked the door. "You got a visitor." He stood me up and put on my handcuffs and helped me shuffle toward the visitor area. I walked into a big open room separated by a large open series of work desks manned by guards and which separated the prisoners from the general public, who looked through a barred window on the other side. One of the guards came over to me and asked, "Are you Handler?"

"Yes."

"You know this guy that's here to see you?" He pointed to the other side of the room and I saw a short guy with shoulder length wavy dark hair, a big mustache and thick glasses. I didn't know him but I definitely was happy to see who he was with. Karol standing next to him smiling and waving.

The guard handed me a folded piece of paper and said, "He handed this to me for you." I opened it up and it read: DON'T TALK TO THESE PIGS. WE NEED TO TALK FIRST. REMEMBER, YOU CAN'T TRUST THEM. I'M EMORY OLMSTEAD, YOUR ATTORNEY. "He's your attorney?"

"I guess so."

"They forget we have to read all messages that come across the desk. He's a piece of work. Good luck, Handler. Joe here will take you to the visitors stations."

Joe sat me at a table next door and I waited for them to join me. This was all starting out to be quite the adventure.

"Alan ... Alan ... Alan ..." Karol repeated when she saw me. "Are you okay? I'm so sorry I ran off, but I didn't know what to do. I knew we needed to find help."

"It's okay. Really. I'm just glad to see you."

"This is Emory. I found him in the yellow pages. He works at a little firm, Masterson and Masterson, downtown. They specialize in drug cases."

We shook hands and all sat.

"Sorry I don't have any business cards to give you,"

Emory began, "This is my first case. I've been at the firm for six months now."

"You ARE a lawyer, right?" I managed to croak out.

"Certainly. Just passed the bar last month. But, in case you're wondering, I really know all about drug cases. In fact, I was where you were sitting a few years ago. So I kind of know it from the inside out."

As I looked at Karol, she glanced down at a table. "So how does this work?"

"The first thing we're going to do is get you out of here. The good news is there's a Drug Defense Fund, which was set up a few years ago by the Grateful Dead when they came through town. They were arrested in South Bend for possession after a concert. They realized too late how strict the laws for drugs are in Indiana. They met a lot of people who didn't have funds to get help. So they decided to help others by covering their cost. We can use those funds to post a bond right now and get you out of here. Once you go to trial and get those dollars back, we put them back in the fund."

"Great. Can you do that soon? I'm more than ready."

"It's happening right now. I posted your bond when I came in. They are preparing paperwork to get you out. Should be just a few minutes." Karol patted my hand. "The rest we can go over in the car when I take you home."

Joe poked his head in. "Okay, Mr. Handler. Time to go bye-bye."

Emory was still talking when he pulled up to our double-wide. "... and I'll call you tomorrow. Get some rest – we have a lot of work to do."

Once inside, I fell on the bed exhausted. I looked at Karol and gave her a big smile and she jumped in bed right next to me. She threw her arms around my neck and whispered in my ear, "I missed you, Handler. I was really worried."

"I missed you too, Karol. I only had an ugly guy named Smitty to keep me warm."

"Shut up and kiss me."

Lying there, next to Karol, was probably one of the happiest moments of my life. I was happy to be alive, happy to be away from that place, happy that I was not a convicted felon (yet) and so happy to be lying next to Karol. It's funny, but even one day of that kind of trauma leaves a mark on you forever. I thought about prisoners who were lifetime criminals and wondered how they stayed sane.

How did they do it?

Just my brief encounter caused me to have flashbacks.

The only other time I felt that way was when I was entered into the first Vietnam War Lottery. When the numbers were pulled by birthday, I had a low one, 108. The day I graduated from LSU, I remember being called in for a physical. My roommate, Jimmy Boudreau, was also called up. He was thrilled. "Hey, Alan ... look at this. I got my letter. I got my letter!"

"Yeah. I got mine too." I said much less gleefully.

"We go on the same day. We can go in together."

Now Jimmy was not athletically inclined. That was being kind. But he loved and studied football. His dream was to somehow get involved with the NFL when he graduated. Not as a player but as a scout or an agent or something. Maybe the word draft excited him. I don't know and I didn't want to burst his bubble. I just smiled and said. "Sure we can go to the

Draft Center together and get our physicals." Which, by the way, we did the following month in New Orleans. There were hundreds of us together dropping our pants and coughing. I remember it well. Hours of exams and questions, not knowing if you passed, failed or got a deferment. Jimmy passed with flying colors in the end. I got a 4F deferment for flat feet. I think 4F meant I could be retested at sometime in case of a national emergency. Apparently flat feet can either get better or not matter eventually. Jimmy was elated but worried about me. "I can't believe they're not taking you, Alan. I'm so sorry man."

"It's really okay, Jimmy. Flat feet are a bitch to march around with."

"Wow, they must be!"

Karol and I talked for hours that night. I opened up about my fears and insecurities. There was a lot to think about now. I worried that maybe this whole incident would become some odd story in the media. "Man gets arrested for possession of marijuana after his car blows up." Not sure how that would play at Everett Finley Academy in La Porte. I can't believe they would want their kids taught by someone associated with drugs. Even if there wasn't a news story about it, how long would it be until the trial started and that would prompt some interest.

Then there was the whole thing about my attorney who never had a case. I knew that beggars couldn't be choosers but … really? I mean, he seemed to know his stuff and he surely had more interest and time to spend I guess. But my life was in his hands. Now that I knew how seriously the people of Indiana took drug possession cases, I was even more worried. What kind of trial would it be? A felony case? Jury?

"Well first we have to get you a car. Maybe a lease huh?" Karol said.

"True. Or we can check the want ads for a cheap used car just for back-and-forth stuff."

"One that doesn't shoot out flames preferably."

"Yeah. Right. And doesn't come with an ounce of weed in the glove compartment."

"Okay. I feel bad enough, Handler. It was all my fault. I told you how sorry I was."

"I know. But I couldn't hear you because you must have whispered it as you left the scene without telling me."

Karol punched me hard in the shoulder. "Stop it."

"Well, at least you found me a lawyer that was fresh out of elementary school. How long did it take you to find that guy?"

"It took me a while, Handler. You know it's not like I had a ton of money to put down on some high-powered attorney. I didn't know where to look, so I was happy to find him."

"He's a handsome little devil isn't he?"

Karol burst into laughter and said, "Well if it's a jury trial we'll find somebody cuter".

"I didn't ask him if we had a court date. Did you?"

"I don't think they set one yet, but he thinks it's not going to be more than a month away. By the way, he told me that the fire chief and the police chief are brothers."

"Oh great. Of course that would be my luck. Let's get some sleep."

At about 8 a.m., Emory Ohlmstead arrived at our door with a big briefcase and a bag of bagels. As I opened the door, he bounded in proclaiming. "I come bearing gifts!"

"Karol just put on some coffee. Would you like some?"

"Yes, yes. Thanks and here are some goodies, too." He handed me the bag as he set his briefcase on the dining room/kitchen table. "I hope you don't mind. I have some paperwork for you and wanted to go over some details."

"No, not at all." I motioned for him to sit as did Karol.

He started pulling out forms and placing them in front for me. "Okay, here's your receipt for the bail money, an attorney contract from our firm that you can look over, a copy of Chief Bill Williams' statement to the police, and here ..." he opened a large manila envelope, "are photos of your vehicle that I took last night at the salvage yard."

I spread out the photos, which were Polaroids of the exterior and interior of the car. Emory pointed to the five pictures of the glove compartment that were taken from every angle possible. "Now, you see these? What is interesting is that you'll notice in these pictures of the glove compartment, the door is hanging loosely on its hinges and damaged as if it was pried loose by a crowbar or something similar."

"Looks like that to me," I said. "I take it that's good for our team?"

"Yes, it is." He brightened. "You see, if they forced open the glove compartment to see what was there and removed it, that would constitute illegal search and seizure. They are legally bound to ask your permission if they have to break it open."

Karol asked, "The fire doesn't change things?"

"No. It's not supposed to. Now they will say it does. That they had to get to wiring or there was an immediate safety concern, but that's shaky ground. And there's the ounce of grass removal question."

"Which is ..."

"They are saying (in Williams' statement) that the grass fell out of the glove compartment onto the floor when they opened the door. VERY tough to prove." Emory smiled as if saying he was VERY proud of himself. "Glove compartments are constructed so that all the items are sitting inside and angled away from the door. In fact there's a lip separating the items from the door frame." He pointed to the picture of the door frame. "For the grass to just fall out would be physically impossible. It had to be removed."

I sat back in my chair. "So that meant that the chief didn't just stumble on it. He caused it to appear."

"Correct!"

Maybe our little lawyer buddy just might be the right guy to get me out of this mess after all.

I called Uncle Benny in Indianapolis.

"Alan ... boychik. You are here in Indianapolis?" I could hear the cheeriness in his voice.

"Well, close by, in South Bend. Teaching school."

"That's great. Come to dinner and stay the night. Jeanette could make a brisket."

"I'd like that. Listen, Uncle Ben, I need your help."

I proceeded to tell him the ballad of the Burning Car without the sad drug ending. As luck would have it, he told me, one of his customers was looking to sell an older Toyota Corolla. He owed Uncle Benny some money from a pawn transaction and would be willing to make him a deal by swapping the car. Benny would be happy to do it and let me have the car for as long as I wanted it.

Karol and I drove to Indianapolis the next day.

Uncle Benny and Aunt Jeanette live in a little suburb of Indianapolis. That day, Jeanette was feeling a little "under the weather," according to Benny, so we opted to meet him at Shapiro's for lunch instead.

"So," Benny said as we sat down to eat the best kosher food in the midwest, "Jeanette sends her love but she's been feeling horrible, just horrible and didn't want to spread her germs."

Karol said, "I hope she gets well soon. I'm sorry I didn't get a chance to meet her."

"And she is sorry she didn't meet you, my dear. She is so good with shiksas … treats them just like family."

Karol tried not to laugh and kicked me under the table.

"Uncle Benny, I really appreciate you letting me take the Toyota for a while. Are you sure it's okay?"

"Don't mention it. My pleasure. Keep it as long as you wish. Enjoy." Benny reached in his pocket. "That reminds me. Here are the keys and here is the address of the lot. The guy in the lot is a guy named Eldin. Nice colored fella who watches merchandise for me. He will take good care of you."

Karol put her head down and chuckled quietly. I kicked her under the table.

"Thanks, Uncle Benny."

"Okay … let's eat," Benny said. "Order whatever you like. Shapiros has been doing this for 100 years, so I think they know what they are doing, huh?"

Karol leaned over to me and whispered, "Alan, what's a gefilte fish?"

I laughed. "Just get a sandwich, babe."

Emory was parked in his old Impala when I pulled up to our place.

He jumped out when he saw us and called out, "Hey, I was in the neighborhood! Got a minute for an update?"

"Sure," I said as I got out of my "new" old Toyota.

"Nice wheels, Alan," Emory said as he stroked the hood.

"My uncle hooked me up."

Karol pulled in just as we reached the front door. "Hi, Emory. Didn't know we were going to have the pleasure of seeing you today."

"Emory has some news for us," I said.

"Good news?" Karol asked.

"Well, not sure." Emory answered.

I looked at him. "Not sure as in … I better get a drink?"

He laughed. "Oh no. Not sure as in: They set a court date. February 4th."

"Emory. That's four months from now."

"I know."

"Our courses end in December, before Christmas."

"I tried to get them to make it earlier."

"What am I supposed to do? Come back?"

"Better if you stay till then. They don't want you to leave the state."

Karol jumped in, "Are the courts that busy?"

Emory shrugged. "Apparently Chief Williams is taking off for a hunting trip in November and the courthouse is closing early for Christmas so they readjusted their schedules."

I was stunned. "But … February 4th?"

"Might be earlier or might be later if they decide to change it." Emory patted my shoulder. "Look, the good news is that they know that they are on shaky ground with search and seizure and I think they are looking for more time to build a case."

Karol interrupted, " Really? Is this a BIG case for them? A bag of pot? Really?"

"They might want to make an example because of the quantity." Emory hesitated and then said, "They might even push for possession and distribution."

"They are gonna say I'm a DEALER?" I said, loud enough for my neighbor to turn his head toward me. I lowered my voice. "Are you serious? Selling this shit? They want to prosecute me for selling this shit."

"Anything over 30 grams puts you in jeopardy. One year for possession and longer for distribution plus a $10,000 fine."

I stood there dumbfounded. JAIL TIME. I never considered jail time until now. I thought a fine, suspended sentence, at home with an iron claw on my ankle but not jail time.

Emory saw my expression. "Don't worry. You're not gonna go to jail. I promise you that."

"How can you be sure?"

"Because they just never prosecute to the fullest in these cases. They want to make an example so they try to scare the shit out of you."

"Yeah? Well it worked!"

"No. Don't worry. I'm gonna make sure you don't do any time. Paying a fine, maybe. But my goal is that they will throw it out completely based on how they arrested you."

I stared at Emory and thought, 'He's gonna save me? The tiny bespectacled, long-haired student who NEVER had a case before?'

I'm fucked.

I was still wide awake at 2 a.m.

My mind was racing. I just stood and stared through the bedroom window and kept envisioning life behind bars. Maybe I'd run into Smitty again. I could be his bitch.

"Come back to bed, baby." Karol sleepily said to me as she turned over in bed.

I continued to stare out the window. "What kind of tattoos should I get for my new home?"

" Well ... my name with a heart for one." Karol got out of bed and put her arms around me from behind. "You are not going to prison, Handler. Emory told you that he is not gonna let that happen."

"He's four feet tall and can't even see. Plus he just passed the bar exam. You really think he can get me off?"

"He's a smart guy. You gotta admit that the strategy he came up with to defend you is pretty damned Perry Mason."

I turned to face her. "Yeah. I have to admit I was impressed." I rested my chin on my hands and admitted, "I'm scared, Karol. I'm really scared."

"Don't worry. We can get through this together."

I felt that pit in my stomach again. Get through this together? Karol didn't have a great track record of doing things together. She was a runner, When the going gets tough, the tough get going ... literally. In our brief history, she had disappeared more than a few times and didn't seem committed to a relationship. Even her words tonight seemed a little hollow. I should say something to her. I should ask her if she's really committed. I'm as bad as she is, afraid to ask and afraid of what she might say. If I were to lose my job over this or, God forbid, go to jail. That would surely be the end of us.

As if she read my mind, her next words were, "Listen Alan, I just want you to know how sorry I am for getting you into this. You've been protecting me from all this horror. It was my pot. I put it in the glove compartment. I should be the one on trial. You have been so great about standing up."

She started to cry. "I'm not good at relationships. Never have been and the ones I tried hard to keep were the ones that eventually hurt the most and left me pretty disappointed and alone. You probably figured that out. Ours has been wonderful. You never ask for more than I can give and – and – well, it kinda scares me that we are moving quickly into something more than I might be able to ..."

I put my fingers on her lips. Then I kissed her. "Let's go to bed."

The ivy-covered buildings on the campus of Finley Academy could have easily been the home to students from Harvard University. The place was massive and beautiful. When I drove through the entrance, a security guard gave me a map and pointed to the administration office, the biggest of the ivy buildings.

This was to be my home for the next eight weeks (unless Indiana State Prison wanted me more).

I sat in Headmaster Jonathan Greely's outer office area,

feeling a little like a bad student sent to the principal's office. A song that I just heard on the radio: *Indiana Wants Me* kept going around in my head. The lyrics were hauntingly ironic: "Indiana wants me. Lord, I can't go back there./ Indiana wants me, Lord I can't go back there."

There's another line in it that goes: "Out there the law's a comin' / I'm gettin' so tired of runin'. Jeez!"

"Mr. Handler?" Jonathan Greely himself greeted me, thankfully interrupting my nightmarish tune.

"That's me," I answered and shook his hand.

"Very nice to have you join our faculty here at Finley. Did you have any trouble finding us?"

"None at all. The directions were perfect." I checked out Greeley's wardrobe and wondered if that was expected of me. Tweed coat replete with the elbow patches, vest and khakis. A bright yellow bowtie topped it off. He was probably in his 40s, I'd guess, thinning blond hair and horn-rimmed glasses. We couldn't have been more different. I tried to straighten out my rumpled wool blazer and adjusted the paisley tie I wore over my white buttoned-down shirt that hadn't been ironed.

"Well, come on in and have a seat." He showed me in and asked, "Coffee?"

"I'm fine." As I sat I looked around and added, "This is a beautiful place."

"Thank you. Thank you. We are very proud of our campus."

"Is Finley the name of a famous person here or was it a benefactor."

"Both, as a matter of fact," Greely said as he handed me a packet embossed with Finley across the top. "Are you familiar with the name Charlie Finley?"

"As in ... owner of the Oakland A's?"

"The very same. Mr. Finley is one of La Porte's most famous residents. We have a few but he's probably the best-known." He paused and leaned across the desk. "Unless you count Belle Gunness, the serial killer who butchered 40 men." He laughed a hearty laugh at his apparently well-practiced joke.

"Did she go to school here too?" I laughed at my joke.

He didn't laugh. "No." After a pregnant pause he continued. "Mr. Finley gifted the school with 90 acres of his sprawling cattle ranch and helped raise the funds for our facilities."

"Very generous."

"Yes it was."

There was a knock on the door and a bearded gentleman with a corduroy suit entered. "Am I too early Jon?"

"Not at all Henry. This is Mr. Handler, our new developmental reading specialist (wow, I liked that title). Mr. Handler, Henry Pippinger, our Academic Dean." We shook hands. "Henry will take you to see your classroom and show you around."

I shook hands with Greeley and thanked him for the opportunity.

Our tour lasted about an hour. I was very impressed with all of it. Even the students, some of whom we saw in the hallways, were so well- behaved and polite. They all wore the Finley uniforms and were all (as far as I could tell) white. I couldn't get over the obvious irony: My first two schools ... Miller was all-black and Finley was all-white. Funny thing, I felt much more at home when I thought about Miller than I did Finley. I think it was the wealth thing. Growing up in a middle-class environment, I didn't socialize with those folks. Instead of insecurity, I felt more anger toward the air of entitlement they carried. I'm sure there was jealousy mixed with the chip on my shoulder, but I was determined to not let that color what I was about to begin.

And then as I visualized myself walking the halls in a prison uniform I started to hum: "Indiana wants me ..." I was relieved to have a normal daytime class schedule for a change. I had two teaching tracks: Juniors and Seniors at 11:30 a.m. (Mondays and Thursdays) for college prep and Freshmen and Sophomores at 2:30 p.m. (Tuesdays and Fridays) for developmental reading skills.

Karol's program already had started in South Bend. Her school was an exclusive all-girls school not too far from the campus of Notre Dame. It too was a beautiful school that catered to the beautiful and wealthy. They loved Karol from the start.

The first Monday of school for me started out a little rocky. My classroom had to be changed and I wasn't given the word. I introduced myself to the students in Room 134 and gave a practiced eloquent speech about our goals for the course. As I finished, teacher Barry Myers, who had been partially hidden by a supply closet door, raised his hand and said, "Mr. Handler. This is my Senior History class, but I am happy to share."

I was mortified.

Barry turned out to be very cool and very helpful. When I finally found out that I was in another building due to a scheduling glitch, I arrived about 10 minutes late. Fortunately, the students were patiently waiting for me, unlike my Miller Academy students when I first had arrived there.

One of my seniors, John Grady, asked if there were assigned seats.

"No, Mr. Grady. You can sit anywhere, but I do want you to sit in the same seat you choose for the rest of the course. That way I can remember your faces and names."

A few students traded seats but most stayed where they were. I took the roll and filled in a makeshift seating chart at the same time. I repeated my eloquent speech to the class and added ... "The students in Senior History have also had the privilege of hearing about our course. They didn't necessarily want to hear it but had no choice when I showed up there this morning by accident."

"Did you see David Friedman?" Marilyn Packer blurted out and then turned bright red. "He's my boyfriend."

"We know. We know," said Toby Davis. Laughter filled the room.

I answered, "Is he a really handsome guy?"

"YES!" she answered.

"Well then, he was definitely there."

After class, a couple of students who either were the class suck-ups or truly overachievers asked me for any preparation materials that they could review. I told them it was not necessary, but I appreciated their conscientiousness.

I jumped into my car and headed to South Bend. Emory asked me to stop by to meet the rest of the team: Masterson and Masterson, I assumed. Karol was going to try to meet me there as well. Her classes were over at 11.

Although I didn't have a preconceived idea about what the building that housed Masterson and Masterson would look like, I was not surprised when I pulled up to a bungalow with a welcoming front porch and a hammock to the left of the front door. I pictured little Emory swinging back and forth as I entered.

A perky receptionist named Miranda welcomed me and asked if she could help me.

"Yes, thanks. I have an appointment with Emory."

"Emory Ohlmstead?"

I looked around at the tiny place. "Are there other Emorys?"

"No. It's just Ohlmstead. Just making sure he's the one you want."

Miranda picked up the phone and I could literally hear Emory in the adjacent room say, "Yes?"

"Mr. Ohlmstead, your next appointment is here."

From the next room, "I'll be right there."

Miranda said, "He will be right ..."

"Yes, I heard him. Thanks."

Emory came booming out of his office with his hand outstretched. "Alan! Let's go back to the conference room. I want you to meet the team."

The conference room was more like the dining room, next to the kitchen. Karol was already there as were two other guys.

"Hi babe," I said as I leaned down to kiss Karol. I turned to the others and added, "I assume you fellas are the Mastersons? Which one of you is Bat?"

They both laughed. "Not like we haven't heard that before. No, neither of us are Mastersons." The shorter of the two replied. "I'm Ira Middleberg and this is my partner Sal Pandolfi."

Karol chuckled as I shook their hands.

Ira continued, "There are no Mastersons. We just thought it sounded like a cool law firm name to put on the shingle. And besides, Middleberg and Pandolfi is a mouthful you know?"

Meeting the two partners did little to add a feeling of confidence of my legal team. Ira looked like an orthodox rabbi in suspenders and Sal looked like Fredo Corleone from The Godfather. Actually, among the three of them sitting there, Emory the untried new attorney, looked the best of all.

"Mr. Handler," Fredo said, "It's a pleasure to meet you and we are honored to be part of your team. We also want you to know that we will use all our resources toward your defense."

I wanted so badly to say ... "It was you, Fredo. You broke my heart." And then grab him on the face and kiss him on the mouth just like Pacino did. But I held back.

Ira jumped in, "Emory has filled us in on everything. The search and seizure defense is one we have used successfully many, many times. This case is very clearly an overextension of the police powers and they know it."

"Do you have any questions for us?"

Karol leaned in and said, "Hey, Sal. Has anyone ever told you that you look like Fredo from The Godfather?"

Karol and I ate at an Italian restaurant that night. After meeting with Fredo, we both had the urge for pasta.

"So what do you think?" Karol asked me after she cut into her ravioli.

"The truth?" I sipped my wine. "I'm glad it's not a jury trial."

Karol laughed, "Low marks on the physical appeal scale for sure. But I think they're all smart guys."

"I don't know." I shook my head. "Know what Fredo told me on the way out?"

"What?"

"I can handle things! I'm smart! Not like everybody says ... like dumb ...I'm smart." I gave the line my best Godfather impersonation.

Karol almost spit up her pasta. "Well ... you think he can convince them to make us an offer we can't refuse?"

I smiled. "Seriously, I think it's gonna be okay. I actually have been feeling much better about Emory. I guess we need to have faith." Karol patted my hand. "So, how have your classes been? Are you liking the school?" I asked her.

"Oh Alan. I love it. The students are bright and a pleasure to teach." She put down her fork. "There is one girl who has really looked to me as a mentor. She's super bright. Her dad is a chemist and her mom works for Delta Air Lines."

"A stewardess?"

"No. She is a pilot. Pretty cool, huh?"

"Yeah," I interrupted. "I don't mean any disrespect, but why is she looking to you as her mentor. She's got some high-powered parents right?"

"Right. I asked her that, in fact. She said her parents, who she loves dearly, are never around. Mom is flying around the world and dad is discovering some new drug every week. She's the youngest of four kids and the other three are all superstars, as well. I think she just wants to talk about life. She wants to get my thoughts on college and dating and other stuff."

"Other stuff?"

"You know ... girl stuff."

"Oh she's a virgin."

"Alan!" She kicks me under the table.

"Hey ... Beggars can't be choosers. I think Emory is single. Or maybe Fredo."

She gave me "the look." You know "the look." Every guy has gotten "the look." It's somewhere between "you are such a child" and "you really are a piece of shit." It didn't deter her from finishing the story and I kept quiet. Karol lit up when she talked about this kid. I got it. I felt the same about my students.

Karol never really wanted to be a teacher. As she told it, she just fell into it, like me. Unlike me, she worked hard at Vanderbilt University. A scholarship student, she worked as a teaching assistant and met her old boyfriend Andy there. Something bad happened. Karol escaped to New Orleans and joined ReadInc.

That's really all I knew.

I didn't even know Andy's last name. She didn't talk about her past at all. Bits and pieces were all I got. Raised by a single mom who was a kindergarten teacher; dad was an abusive alcoholic who died young, her brother was manic depressive.

She was the one constant in their lives, apparently, committed to taking care of them both. This, of course, made her even more attractive to me and at the same time more of an enigma. I wanted to know more and even help if I could and she was intent on keeping that part of her life private.

As if she read my mind again she stopped her story and said, "By the way, I don't know if I told you that Kelly was readmitted to the hospital yesterday."

"No. Sorry to hear that."

"I may have to take another trip to Mississippi."

The clouds came and our conversation ended.

Finley's teachers lounge was standing room only when I got there at noon. Barry Myers, my friend from senior history, was sitting on the couch with me. I asked him why the lounge was so crowded.

"I'll show you." Barry stood and called to the Art teacher, Johnna Roberts. "Johnna, I want you to meet Alan Handler. He's the new reading specialist. Alan, this is Johnna Roberts, our fantastic art teacher"

Johnna was ... I would guess in her early 30s, a redhead, very well endowed, micro mini skirt and gorgeous. "Nice to meet you, Alan." She smiled and winked. "Welcome to Finley."

"Thank you, Miss Roberts. Nice to be here."

"It's Johnna. Even my mother doesn't want to be called Miss Roberts." She shook my hand. "Well, boys. Time to go. My students await."

As she walked away, I said to Barry. "I get it. I definitely get it."

"It's like clockwork. This is her break time and when she leaves, there are plenty of seats in the house." Sure enough, the male faculty members assembled started to leave the lounge one by one. "So Alan, how are you liking the place so far?"

"Today was a good day!"

Barry agreed. "Where are you living?"

"My girlfriend and I have a place in South Bend. She

teaches at Harris Women's Academy." That was the first time I referred to Karol as my girlfriend. Actually, the first time I referred to her at all. I wondered what she would say if she heard that.

"Your girlfriend's here? That's cool."

"What about you, Barry?"

"Wife and two little ones. We live in Michigan City where, believe it or not, I grew up." He laughed at himself. "Let me correct that. I should have said where I spent my childhood. I have never grown up."

"I resemble that."

"You and your girlfriend should come over some night. My wife is a damned good cook."

"That would be great." I liked Barry. He was a down-to-earth kinda guy. I knew Karol would like him too. His wife was probably cool, I guessed. But I'd been wrong about that before. Unfortunately it was rare to find a couple who were good to hang with. And no one thinks of themselves as socially unacceptable. Of course, there were exceptions. Karol and I were both very cool to hang with ... if I do say so myself.

Emory showed up at six, He had become a regular visitor to our double-wide. Having an apparent dislike for telephones, he much preferred unscheduled drop-ins.

"'What a surprise, Emory," I said as I opened the door before he knocked.

"You know, I was in the area and I thought I'd just see if you were busy." He walked right in lugging his big briefcase. "I have VERY interesting news."

Karol had walked in just as I motioned to Emory to sit down.

He continued, "I have a friend in the Fire Department that told me that the chief had a massive heart attack the first day of his hunting trip. He's currently in Michigan City Hospital in critical condition."

I looked at Karol and we both turned to Emory in an accidental but perfectly timed double-take.

"So," Emory said as he took out a few documents. "He is the main witness ... actually in our search and seizure defense ... the only witness. Without him, they have a hard time countering our claim."

"How do you like your steak, Emory?" Karol asked.

Every night, it seemed I had the same recurring dream. I was in a jail cell, naked, with Smitty sitting next to me and staring at a huge toilet in the middle of the cell. Emory was sitting on top of the toilet, going through documents. I dreamt the same dream that night with an additional part. Chief Williams was in the adjoining cell hooked up to an IV when suddenly his bed burst into flames causing a fire throughout the jail. When the flames reached my feet, I woke up.

I bolted upright. It was 3 a.m. and Karol was not lying next to me.

In the darkness I saw her silhouette leaning on the window and staring out into space, She had a half-smoked joint in her right hand and a glass of wine in the left. "Hey," I said. "You okay?"

"You were moaning in your sleep."

"Sorry. Did I wake you up?"

Karol kept looking outside. "You know, when I was a little girl, my dad used to wake me up in the middle of the night while my mother slept. He would crawl into my bed. What happened next is a total blank to me now." She took a long sip of her wine. "But I remember staring at all the stars for a long time after he left. I would fly so high ... just drifting in space and eventually land in a place that I had never been. It was a place that was so calm and beautiful."

I watched her as tears fell from her cheeks and shared in her grief as I too began to cry.

Thursday night was the night we were invited to go to Barry and Isabel Myers' place for dinner. But a lot had transpired since then. Karol was still not herself since she heard the news about her brother Kelly. In fact she had taken a few days off of school – which was difficult due to the short turnaround schedule. We had good news from Emory. It seemed things were turning in my favor. But things were emotional at home.

"Karol, you sure you want to do this tonight?" I asked her as we were getting dressed. "Barry seems like the kinda guy who would understand if we rescheduled."

"I don't want to do that to them," she answered. "Isabel has probably put a lot of work into cooking and cleaning the house. It's only two hours notice."

"But if we said you were sick tonight and ..."

"No, Handler. We are going."

We finished dressing in silence and didn't really speak on the hour-long drive over. I stopped to pick up a bottle of wine that I only hoped and prayed they would like, and it wasn't the usual rot-gut stuff I typically pick ... because I have no idea what good wine should be like. I figured if there wasn't a picture of Boone's Farm on the label, it should be acceptable.

We pulled up to the house and stepped up to the door.

Both Barry and Isabel greeted us at the front door. "Welcome, guys!"

"Hey. Thanks for letting us into this beautiful neighborhood and taking a chance on reducing your property value."

"Oh ... I did that years ago according to my neighbors."

We all made our introductions at the front door and were ushered inside to the den. "How about some wine?"

I handed him my gift. "I just so happen to have this for you."

The house was just what I expected from a history professor. Very comfortable, lots of bookshelves, antique furniture ... the kind that's not really ornate and hard to sit in.

"So where are the kids?" I asked Isabel.

"Oh we threw them out of the house earlier. They kept begging to come back but we said go find work or something."

Karol broke into a big grin. "It's a lot of work, huh?"

"Yes. But they are little loves." Isabel broke out the photo album. "Here is Katherine ... no hair ... big grin ... sweetest little thing until she's hungry, or tired, or mad, or needy ..."

"So is that never?" Karol asked.

"Right! Oh, maybe asleep. Yes, when she's asleep she's so sweet. And this is Georgie. He is always sweet. Truly."

"Beautiful kids. I know people are supposed to say that, but these two are really beautiful." Karol said.

"Thanks. My sister is watching them tonight so we can

have some adult time."

Barry came back with wine and cheese and crackers. "So what do adults talk about these days?"

I scratched my head. "Ummm Nixon, moon walk, streaking ..."

"Wait a minute! Somebody walked on the moon?" Barry asked. "Amazing. And ... Who's Nixon?"

Karol piped in, "You didn't mention streaking."

Isabel said, "We know all about that. We've got two kids remember? They invented it."

"Usually with something dragging behind them coming from their butts." Barry stopped himself. "See that? See what we did? We changed the subject back to kids. It's a bad habit."

"We don't mind not talking about Nixon," Karol said.

After a few glasses of wine and a great dinner, we were all a little loose. Barry asked if we were game players and of course we immediately jumped at the chance and he said, "What about Charades? Girls against the boys?"

"Oh lord," said Isabel. "Karol, I'm really not great. I don't know if you want me for a partner. English is my second language."

"Don't be silly. We will rule these guys." Karol sat next to Isabel. "Is Spanish your first language?"

"I was born in Colombia. But my first language these days is gaga googoo."

Barry grabbed some paper and pencils and handed them out. "Okay. Write down five movie titles, five book titles and five famous people. Rip them into strips and fold them. Then we'll make two stacks ... one for the guys and one for the girls."

Isabel whispered to Karol. "Oh, this will be easy. We will

already know our answers."

Karol laughed. "No, sweetie. The boys will do our stack and we will do theirs."

"Oh. See what I mean, Karol? I am a terrible charades partner." Karol patted her knee.

Karol jumped up after the stacks were finished. "Can I go first?"

Barry grabbed the stopwatch. "Sure. You've got three minutes."

Karol picked up her piece of paper, opened it and read to herself, Exodus. She looked down at Isabel. "Ready?"

"Yes." Isabel said.

"Go." Said Barry.

Karol did the gesture for "book".

"Um ... READ!" Isabel said.

Karol shook her head. She did it again.

"READ A BOOK?"

"No. That means it's a book title," she said.

"No talking," I joked with her.

"Hush up, Handler. It's just the reference."

Karol held up her finger.

"ONE?" Isabel said. "ONE WORD!"

Karol nodded. She put three fingers on her arm to show how many syllables. Isabel didn't get it.

"THREE ... um VEINS ... um ARMS ... um ..."

"SYLLABLES," Karol finally said. "One word and Three syllables."

Before I could open my mouth, Karol gave me THE LOOK. So I said. "Okay ... we will let that slide."

She put one finger out on her arm and then did the sign

for "x"

"X!"

Karol shook her head and smiled at Isabel like she had just won the lottery. She did the second syllable and formed an "o" with her fingers. Isabel got it. "X! O!"

The third syllable was harder. Karol tried a lot of clues, but none stuck until she came to "dust" pantomiming dusting a shelf. Isabel got it immediately. By that time however, time was running out and "x-o-dust" was not gonna become Exodus.

"ZZZZZZ"– Barry made the buzzer sound for times up. "Sorry ladies. Good try, though."

"Karol … I'm sorry." Isabel said.

"Don't worry. We are gonna win."

The next round didn't go too well for the girls either. Isabel had to do Cool Hand Luke and she was all over the place. By the fourth round we were well ahead. Karol was so competitive that I knew this was killing her. Isabel was so cute and so lost, but had a great sense of humor. Barry and I were really rubbing it in. "The men rock! We cannot be beaten! Guys rule!" And other obnoxious stuff. Everyone was having a great time … I thought.

On my next turn I stood up to do Wizard of Oz and accidentally said to Barry, "MOVIE!" Karol stood up and yelled at me. "NO TALKING."

We all sat back in our seats stunned. "Sorry. Let me start again."

I did the sign for movie and Karol again said, "No. You lose a point and you lose your turn. That's the rule."

"C'mon. You weren't penalized when you did it. It's just

the descriptor."

"That's different. Isabel didn't know the signs and the rules. You do."

"Karol, it's okay. We are so far behind …" Isabel started to say.

"THAT IS NOT THE POINT. If you don't follow the rules you lose a point."

You could have heard a pin drop.

"You know, I am not going to play anymore. Handler! You are being totally unfair to me and to Isabel. Our clues were much harder and you seem to just make up your own rules as you go along. I'm taking the car Handler. I am so sorry, Barry and Isabel. You have a lovely home and served a lovely dinner."

I stood and tried to get her to sit. "Honey. Please let's just …:"

"NO."

Remember when I said that it's rare to have couples who are compatible with each other and Karol and I were the exception?

I was wrong.

Barry had offered to take me for a drink and then a ride home. I took him up on it.

He racked the balls on the pool table in his favorite bar, O'Malley's. I couldn't focus on anything but the horrible scene played out by Karol just an hour earlier. What the hell was that all about? I know Barry wanted to ask the same thing but was nice enough to keep the conversation from going there.

"So tell me about this program of yours. It's geared

toward reading comprehension and college prep?"

"Pretty much. There are exercises to get kids to read with the purpose of hitting key words and concepts, which increases their speed and gives them more confidence and focus. Helps in test-taking as well. It actually works for most students. Of course they have to want to do it."

I won the break and slammed the balls with my first stroke a little too hard that scattered the balls without getting any in the pockets. Big surprise.

"Easy, big guy. You had your balls broken once all ready tonight."

We both laughed. It broke the ice and actually felt good.

"Crazy shit, Barry. It's crazy shit."

"Hey ... we have all had our balls broken, my friend. That's why God gave them to us, I guess."

"Well mine have had their share this year for sure."

Barry hit the number six ball in the right corner. "How long have you guys been together?"

"A few months. Met her in training classes and we really clicked right away. She's really something special – when her head isn't exploding. I'm really sorry you guys had to see her like that."

"Beautiful girl and obviously bright." Barry finished me off with a tough eight ball shot in the side pocket.

We put the sticks down and sat at the bar. The owner was either a big fan of Notre Dame or an alum. There was memorabilia everywhere. Helmets, signed footballs, pictures of the ND greats. Over the bar was a huge printed sign that read "THIS ONE'S FOR THE GIPPER", a reference to the great Knute Rockne and the Ronald Reagan movie. "Were you a

Notre Dame guy?"

"Nah. I went to Indiana in Bloomington. I'm a public school boy." Barry called the bartender over. "Two more of the same."

"I always thought Notre Dame must have been the coolest place when I was growing up watching the games on TV, you know?"

"They had TV sets down south?"

"Yeah, but we didn't figure out how to use them until a few years ago." I grinned and sipped my newly poured beer. "Asshole."

Barry was one of those rare people who made you feel like you've known him all your life. Sitting there at O'Malley's made me temporarily forget my legal troubles, my Karol troubles, my car troubles ... Amazing what a few beers with the right person can do.

"Hey, Barry. I've been meaning to talk to you about an idea I had for you."

"No, Alan. I am not leaving Isabel for Karol."

"Shut up, man. Seriously. It's about teaching."

"Okay. Lay it on me." He took one long sip from his beer.

"You teach middle school kids, too, right?"

"Yeah. I have a unit in Civics and Social Studies for seventh graders."

I pushed out my stool and stood next to him to explain. "I thought about this at my last school and the idea would be better suited for middle school. Kids respond to stuff that is relevant for them, right?"

"Right."

"No surprise, I know, but I had this idea that day-to-day stuff is not taught in school. Curriculum is geared toward concepts that sometimes can't be applied to their own lives." I laid out two stacks of napkins. "So I thought maybe you could build a community in the classroom. Each kid would pick a job from a group of occupations that either you decide on based on class size. Like doctor, lawyer, banker, mechanic, plumber, etc." I picked up one of the napkins and said, "Then each kid picks a random card with the job and a description on it. They take that job seriously and research what their role is in that community: how much they get paid, if they pay a lease on their business, etcetera."

"You put a lot of thought into this, big guy."

"That's just the beginning. Once you have the basic community, they can do other stuff. They can look for houses and see what they can afford and then pick out carpeting, fixtures and stuff. They can get married – virtually I mean. And have a Town Council that they participate in." I picked up another stack of napkins. "At the Council meetings, you would pick a card that has different challenges for them to tackle as a group, like voting on taxes or elections – you know?"

"Fantastic. But there's one problem my friend."

"What's that?"

"When am I gonna teach the other stuff they need to learn? The school curriculum."

I sat back down. "I haven't figured that part out. But if you could carve out even 15 minutes in every class for Community time I think it would be cool."

It was Barry's turn to stand and finish his beer. "Alan, I love that idea. I think it just might be able to be done and you're the guy to team up with. We can do it together."

"Really?"

"Really. Let's get together tomorrow in the Johnna Roberts Teachers Lounge."

I got home around 2:30 a.m. Barry and I were both buzzed. He was in no shape to drive all the way to South Bend so I thanked him for everything and grabbed a cab.

Karol was fast asleep.

I wasn't tired and still kinda pumped about sharing my Community idea with Barry. I took out my portable typewriter and started to bang out some more ideas for the project and organize my thoughts. As I wrote, I realized how much I enjoyed the process, the whole process of writing and creating something out of nothing. I had always wanted to write the great American novel one day. I started a draft when I was at LSU. Maybe I'll dust that off soon.

Karol stirred and turned over in bed.

I thought to myself, "If I live through my 20s, I'll have lots of rich material to write about for sure."

I woke up in the same position I was in the night before. The only difference was that my head was resting on the typewriter keys. I think it was my head. I really had no feeling from the neck up, although my neck had enough feeling for my whole body. It screamed in pain as I did when I sat up.

Karol was not there when I glanced at the bed. The bed was made and looked like no one had slept in it. On the table next to me was a covered plate with silverware and a napkin next to it. There was a letter sitting right on top.

I stared at the envelope and felt the same rush of

nervousness I did when colleges sent me acceptance/rejection letters. I was in no hurry to open this one because I thought I would not like the outcome. Rejection hurts.

I did lift the lid on the covered plate first and saw that it was a bagel and cream cheese, a nice array of sliced fruit and a couple of slices of bacon. "Last meal," I supposed.

As I bit into the bagel, I opened the letter and began to read:

> *Handler ... I'm ashamed. I couldn't face you this morning. I am so sorry for the way I acted. I don't know what came over me. Shitty day yesterday, but that's no excuse. I behaved badly and ruined a perfectly wonderful night. You deserve better than this ... than me. I had to leave early for classes. There's only a week left with my program and I need to spend time wrapping up. Would you go on a date with me tonight? I can meet you at our favorite Italian restaurant at 6. Afterward I'll make it worth your while. XXXOOO KRB*
>
> *PS ... I will call Isabel this morning and apologize profusely.*

"Wow. Hell of an acceptance letter," I thought. One more puzzle piece in the life of Karol Rae that just didn't seem to fit any corner. I was relieved that she decided to stay but I admit, the stress of not knowing who was going to be there when I got home or even at the restaurant tonight was wearing on me. I didn't know much about mental illness. Once I read that manic depressive symptoms include trouble sleeping, mood changes, but that's all I really knew and frankly if that was the case, I could be that, too. Karol was certainly on the extreme end of this and I was very concerned.

I saw a book that Karol kept close at hand, sitting next

FOR THOSE WHO CAN

to the bed: *Living With Mental Illness*. I tucked it into my book bag and finished my breakfast.

When I saw Barry in the Teachers Lounge, he was sitting right next to Johnna the knockout Art teacher. I grabbed the chair next to him.

"Well, here is the famous Mr. Handler now!" Johnna said as I sat down. "Alan, Barry was just telling me about the fabulous idea you have for middle-school students studying social studies. Can't wait to see how this comes together."

"Um. Thanks. Yeah ... I hope so."

"Oh, it will. I'm sure of it." Johnna stands. "Well, I'll leave you two to talk. Nature calls."

"Bye, Johnna." I turned to Barry as she exited. "Every time I see her she heads to the bathroom. Is it me?"

"No, buddy, she's young, you know. Her kidneys are probably still in development."

I opened my bag. "I've got some stuff for you to look at."

Barry looked through the notes. "Holy shit, Handler! You did all this last night? When? At 4 in the morning?"

"Nah ... I think it was about 4:30."

As Barry perused the pages he said, "I had another thought. Economics is part of my curriculum and I was thinking that we might incorporate banking and the stock market as well. You know, kids can manage checking and savings accounts and pick stocks."

"That's a great idea, man. And it's an exercise they can bring home."

I pulled out a series of index cards from my bag. "I started to come up with some Community cards like this one:

'Sanitation has been an issue. The Community needs a plan of action for trash pickup and maintenance. Another jobs creation and tax discussion.' I've got one for library, postal service and police as well."

Barry put the papers down. "Okay, I say we do this in stages. You are here for another two weeks, right?" I nodded. "So you and I present it to my seventh graders and get them started with basics like job creation, naming the town, elections, and town council meetings. When you have to go, I'll keep it going with phase two, researching homes and opening accounts. My class can be our template and research lab for development. This could be big, my friend. And you and I will be partners." He paused and looked at me. "That is, if you want to do it that way. I was assuming ..."

"Barry, I couldn't be happier with that. I had just wanted to give it to you and let you run with it so I could watch it grow. I'm just a reading teacher with a half finished novel. But I'd love to be part of this thing with you."

"That's a deal!" Barry extended his hand and we shook on it. I loved that Barry was so pumped about this idea. I started to wish that I was going to be there longer. I really didn't want to leave, but I knew that my next assignment was going to be sent soon.

"Hey, by the way, Karol called Isabel this morning."

"She did? She told me she was going to."

"Isabel was happy. She had felt badly that things fell apart and blamed herself for being a ding dong at charades. But Karol took the bullet. It was a very nice thing to do."

"It was also the right thing to do. I'm glad she did it."

"Did you talk to her about it?"

"She was asleep when I got home so I didn't wake her and

she left before I got up but she left me a note … asked me out on a date tonight at our favorite Italian restaurant and told me she was gonna call you guys."

"That's cool."

I decided to trust Barry with a very personal story. "You know, I had the strangest dream last night."

"Wait a minute. Is this gonna get kinky? No chains and leather right?"

"Nah. Just a whip or two." I was glad that I had Barry to talk to. I really wanted to share my frustration with somebody and couldn't say these things with many people. "I dreamed Karol was sitting in the corner crying. She held a teddy bear just like a child. I walked over to her and reached for the light, but she stopped me from turning it on. She said, 'I'm afraid.' I asked her if she was afraid of the dark. In my dream, her voice sounded like it was almost surreal and pretty damned scary. She said, 'No. I AM THE DARK. I'm afraid of … THE LIGHT.' So I asked her why she was afraid of the light. She stopped crying and stood eye-to-eye with me. 'Because light consumes the dark.' Just like that. She said it just like that. Then I woke up with my face planted in my typewriter from the night before."

"That's heavy shit, man. I think I want to hear the whips and kinky stuff instead."

"It is heavy – huh! I thought about it all morning and I think I figured out the deeper meaning. Her brother has been hospitalized for bipolar disorder and I know Karol worries that she might have the same thing. The 'dark' is that place that she thinks she's not only in, but that she's become. And the 'light' is the realization that she has a mental condition that will handicap her for the rest of her life."

"Can you get her some help?"

"We don't really talk about any of this stuff. Well, at least we don't talk about her issues. She brushes over it and focuses mostly on Kelly, her brother. I don't know how she'd take it if I brought this up and offered help."

"You think she might be ... like ... a danger to herself?"

"I don't know. I thought about maybe calling her mom. But I never met her and I don't even know how to get in touch with her. Plus – that might really piss Karol off and send her over the deep end."

I looked at my watch.

"Gotta go, huh?" Barry said.

"Yeah. Sorry to bend your ear on this."

"Don't be stupid. That's what friends are for. I just wish I could help, but I've only got a wife and two kids."

I patted Barry on the back. "That's why I asked. You can handle anything. Hey let's set a date for Community release, okay?"

"You got it."

I left the school later than usual, and headed to our Italian Restaurant to meet Karol. I had decided to spend time working on projects in The Teachers' Lounge instead of going back to the doublewide first. I felt the need to be as busy as I could with numerous projects to keep my mind off of other present issues. I even got a few pages of my novel written.

Karol's car was there. It was early and I felt like a senior citizen heading into the early-bird special universe. When I walked in, Karol gave me the sweetest smile and wave. God, I wish it could always be like this.

"Hey there, good-looking," I said as I gave her a kiss and took my seat.

"Back at ya, handsome."

From behind me, I heard the sound of familiar shuffling feet. When I looked up, there was Emory Ohlmstead himself. Before I could say a word, Emory said, "Don't worry. I'm not staying for dinner."

"That's a relief," I joked.

"I brought you this." Emory put a bottle of wine on the table. "And dinner is on me! Well ... on Masterson and Masterson."

"Really?" I said. "And to what do we owe the pleasure?"

"Drum roll," Emory said as he did a little patter on the table with his hands. "Your case ... has been dropped!"

I sat there with my jaw opened in silence.

Karol added, "Emory called me yesterday with the news and I said let's wait to tell you when we can celebrate ... and tonight... we celebrate!"

"What? This is fantastic." I was stunned. "Tell me more ... How? When?"

Emory said, "Well, the Fire Chief, Bill Williams, did pass away this past week. The city attorney, in concert with the police chief, knew this case was up for review. They made the decision to drop the charges because I think they were worried about going to court without the fire chief and didn't want to open up the search and seizure issue without him. So ... you are a free man!"

I hugged the little fella right there in the middle of the restaurant and kissed him on top of his head. "You are the best, Emory. And be sure to tell Fredo and the rabbi how much we appreciate them too."

"Who?"

"Not important, Emory," Karol added. "Thanks for everything. And for dinner. Are you sure you don't want to stay?"

"Yes, I am sure ... this is your night! Enjoy." Emory strode off.

"What a relief!" I reached over and picked up the bottle of wine. Before I even got the words out, a server took it from my hands and offered to open it for us. She deftly opened the bottle and poured out two good-sized glasses of wine and announced that she would be back to get our order.

I took a long sip and said, "Wow. I feel like a big load has been lifted from my shoulders."

Karol reached over and grabbed my hand and looked into my eyes. It was a look of kindness and love. Amazing. The shift in personality was right there in her eyes. The night before the look in those same eyes was one of hatred and blame. I know we all have the ability to change our looks and to have a wide range of emotions, but for me, it has always been hard to fake the love emotion. Not only by verbalizing it but by showing it ... truly showing it. Anger is much easier and harder to control. But the eyes tell the story. Karol's story was certainly a complicated one.

"Wanna talk about last night?" I asked.

The eyes changed. The expression stayed kind and loving but I swear, the eyes changed. "I don't suppose we can forgive and forget," she said. "Can we?"

"Is that what you want me to do?"

Karol picked up her glass, took a sip and sat back. "I want

to be able to talk about this as honestly as I know how."

"Okay. So tell me. What happened?"

"I can't."

"You can't?" It was impossible to hide my frustration. "You CAN'T or you WON'T?"

"I can't. Because I don't remember what I did." Karol now leaned in toward me and lowered her voice to almost a whisper. "Handler, I blocked it all out this morning. In fact, I think I physically blocked it out while I was saying or doing what I did last night."

"I don't understand."

"I know it sounds weird, but I've done it before. It's like blackouts but it happens when I'm awake. I KNOW I did something offensive and I have a visual reference of that but what I did and what I said are ... gone."

I finished off my wine and sat in silence. I had heard of murderers blacking out while they stabbed their victims 50 times. I always thought that was a little bit of bullshit to help their defense. But this? There was no real trauma, just plain old anger and self-righteousness.

"Handler," she continued. "I wouldn't blame you if you wanted to just call it quits. I'm the one with all the baggage. I can't seem to get out of my own way. And my family ..."

"I don't want to give up on you. On us. I just want to understand and to help."

"You can't help. Others have tried and I know I'm a hopeless case. My genetics are working against me and I have a history. I have a long history."

"Let's get you help then. Professional help, if you think you need it."

"No. I've seen what that does NOT do. Kelly is not getting better, He is getting worse with the drugs and treatment and I don't want that."

"But you don't know that Kelly has what you have."

"NO!" Eyes were now on us. Karol lowered her voice. "No, Handler. I just want to try to manage and live my semi-normal life. Are you okay with that?"

"If that's how you want it." This new revelation was really shocking to me. It answered some of the questions I had about her stability, unfortunately. For the time being, I committed to being there. But I truly didn't know if it would be enough for her. Or for me, to be frank. "I'm here."

She kissed me.

The next morning, I slept in. I didn't set the alarm at all. No classes for me and Karol's program had ended. After a big dinner, we made love and Karol fell asleep in my arms. I think it was the first really good night of sleep that I had since we got to South Bend.

When I woke up, Karol was standing over me, smiling. She was wearing her navy peacoat, knitted hat and gloves. "You are so pretty," she told me.

"I'm pretty?" I asked and smiled back. "No ... YOU are pretty."

"When you sleep, you're pretty."

"Pretty tired," I said. "You going somewhere?"

"Yes. Going home to be with the family. Worried about my mom and Kelly."

"Let me help you with your bags," I said as I started to get up.

"No. You stay in bed and sleep. I already put them in my car."

"How long are you gonna be gone?" I asked.

"Don't know. I'll call you from my mom's house, okay?"

"Okay."

She bent down and gave me a passionate kiss, the kind of kiss that's more than a so-long kiss. It was a goodbye kiss.

Karol was not coming back.

FOR THOSE WHO CAN

CHAPTER FOUR

Sadness and Elation

I got a call from Tommy Thompson after Karol had sent in her letter of resignation. He couldn't understand why she decided to leave right in the middle of the school year and after she had had only one assignment.

"Join the club, Mr. T." I was just getting back from closing out my classes on my last day. "I know there are family issues and she was going home to see her family but have no clue why she quit her job."

"Strange. Well, since you're flying solo, I have an assignment that just came up and it's short-term. It requires only one teacher. St. Christopher's in Gary, Indiana."

"Like the song?"

"What song?"

"You know … from *The Music Man*. 'Gary Indiana Gary Indiana Gary Indiana …' "

"Handler, you ever been to Gary, Indiana?"

"Nope. Is it nice?"

"It's … close by."

It's close by. That didn't sound too promising.

The good thing was that Gary was less than an hour's drive to La Porte and I could come back and forth to visit Barry and work on our Community program. The program was getting great reviews from students. From the very first day we presented it, they loved everything about it so far. And they worked hard on every assignment: researching salaries, finding information about real estate, interacting in town halls. All turned out better than I imagined. The biggest problem was having the students focus on the other curriculum. Barry wasn't concerned. I think he wanted to just find a happy balance.

I was happy for the distraction. Karol threw me for a loop. I was still reeling from her yoyo emotional roller coaster and sudden departure, although I have to admit, I wasn't surprised. And what was left of the sane part of my life was a little relieved that she was gone.

We guys have pretty fragile egos, although we don't like to admit it. After she left, there were days that I questioned what I did wrong. How could she leave ME? I was supposed to leave HER. She didn't feel as strongly about me as I did about her. I had invested in this relationship and she didn't. Oh my God ... I was turning into my mother.

Gary, Indiana was certainly close by, as Tommy Thompson said and I understood why he didn't go any further than that. It was a cold, drearily gray place. The road leading to the school was lined with black slush from occasional snowfalls that apparently were not white and fluffy.

The city was founded by US Steel Corporation in the early 1900s. It was the home of the world's largest steel plant, Gary Works, and named for lawyer Elbert Henry Gary, founding chairman of US Steel. As with many cities in the Rust Belt, Gary's rise and fall are reflective of the steel industry.

Gary is only 25 miles from Chicago but far from being a bedroom community of that city. Its residents were largely foreign-born Eastern Europeans and at its peak, the population was over 150,000. The decline started in the early 60's, when growing competitiveness in the steel industry caused US Steel to create numerous layoffs. The crime rate and the closures of businesses continued over the coming years. Gary was destined to be a forgotten city.

My contact at St. Christopher's was the principal, a very jovial priest named Father Stanley Kowolski. He was in his late 60s I guessed, wore horn-rimmed glasses and a broad smile.

Father Kowolski had a welcoming office and, ironically, a very severe, humorless secretary named Mrs. Jones, who took her job very seriously and apparently protected Father Kowolski from those who would take advantage of him.

"What time was your appointment, Mr. Handler?"

"Oh. I didn't have an appointment ma'am," I said to Mrs. Jones. "But I know that Father Kowolski wanted me to arrive today."

"I'm sure that you understand that Father Kowolski has a very busy agenda so I will check with him." She disappeared into his office and then back again quickly. "You may come in."

He met me in the doorway. "Mr. Handler. How very nice to meet you. Thank you for coming here so quickly."

We shook hands. "Very nice to meet you too, Father."

He offered me a seat at his small office table and poured me some coffee. "Mr. Handler, I'm not sure how much you know about us here at St. Chris."

"I read a briefing paper about the history of the school and a little about the city," I said as I reached into my book bag to get it out.

"Good. Good. Well, you might have read that we are a small school and that we have a population that unfortunately has many needs. Families are split, unemployed, and the kids … well … they suffer the consequences."

Father Kowolski took out a tablet that he had scribbled some notes on. "I had heard good things about the programs that ReadInc delivers and I made the call a month ago to try to get things started. So … long story short … we have about 10 seniors here that I think could really benefit from taking this program."

"Great. That would be a perfect-sized class to get some one-on-one work done."

"Good. Good. Now I want to ask you a personal favor."

"What can I do for you?"

"These students have no money and I wanted to do something special for them."

"If it's scholarship dollars, I think that's better discussed with Mr. Tom Thompson. I can get you in touch …"

"No. Not about scholarships. I've talked to Mr. Thompson. I know there are no scholarships per se. I want to pay for these students personally."

"Well, that is very generous, sir. I'm sure the families will be very grateful."

"Oh no no no. That's why I am asking you this favor. They shouldn't know about this. You see, our folks are very proud and would not want to take charity. I want to give you the cash and have you handle all the bookkeeping away from the school. As far as they are to know, the tuition has been taken care of. No need to tell them how or who just that it has been done so they feel comfortable. Is that acceptable?"

"Certainly. I can help you with that."

Father Kowolski rose quickly and held out his hand. "Very good. We will have a classroom ready for you on Monday at 1:00 p.m.. Does that work?"

"Perfect," I said as I shook his hand and he ushered me out.

What a special guy. He obviously loved his kids and would do anything for them. I can't believe that priests get paid a salary large enough to pick up a tuition tab like that. In fact, I didn't know they got paid at all. And to think that he is willing to spend it on the kids and do it anonymously.

As I walked across the parking lot I passed a little VW beetle that had seen better days. The parking sign in front of it read: Father K, Principal.

Definitely, my new hero.

Barry was waiting for me in the parking lot of Finley Academy where I pulled up. "Hop in, partner."

He threw a big briefcase in the back seat and then joined me up front. "Tell me this guy's name again."

"Emory Ohlmstead. And I have to warn you, he just started practicing law ... he's pretty young and he's a weird-looking dude."

"I'm feeling more and more confident every minute that he's the guy to help us protect our Community Program." Barry laughed.

"I know. I said the same thing when I first met him, but he is someone that I have learned to trust and admire."

"And where did you meet this guy?"

I told him about the Ballad of the Burning Car and Ounce of Grass. Arlo Guthrie would have been proud.

"You're serious?"

"Dead serious. Actually, dead is a good description of how I felt at times."

"You were going through all that and teaching, too?"

"Yep. And trying to maintain sanity at home." There was a light flurry of snow mixed with rain coming down so I turned on the wipers. "Emory saved my ass. I owe him."

"I guess you do!"

"But listen. That's why I set this meeting up for both of us. I want you to meet him and then we can decide. I made no promises to Emory. I'm not even sure he can do what we are asking. But I trust him. He's honest and loyal."

"Sounds good."

Barry took out some student papers from his briefcase. "You mind if I grade some tests?"

"Not at all."

My favorite receptionist greeted us as we entered. "Good afternoon Mr. Handler," Miranda said, cheerily as always. "Mr. Ohlmstead is expecting you."

"Thanks, Miranda."

Emory peeked out of his office when he heard my voice. He stepped out to the front. "Hey, Alan. How are you?"

I reached out my hand, but Emory gave me a bear hug instead.

"Emory, this is my good friend and teaching partner, Barry Myers."

"I rarely hug on the first date," Barry held out his hand,

Emory broke into a huge grin and shook his hand. "Very nice to meet you. Let's go into the conference room."

Barry took out three folders – one for each of us – filled with information that he had organized and assembled detailing the Community Program as it stood. I added a little color to the conversation and we both gave our vision for the future. "So, Emory, basically we are looking to protect the program, if there is a chance there is future income we might get for it. You know? If we sell it or franchise it or whatever. We need advice."

Emory was uncharacteristically quiet throughout the presentation. He studied his folder for a few minutes and then said, "This is fantastic, guys. I gotta say, I've never heard of anything like it being taught in school and it's stuff the kids probably love. I would!"

"Thanks, Emory," I said. "They really do like it and they're learning a lot."

"So the way I see it, you need legal help in setting up the partnership model and in protecting your intellectual property," he said, then paused a minute. "I have been working on the criminal law side since I've been at Masterson, but my area of study is really corporate law, so I can help you on the business setup and structures. The protections are usually handled by attorneys who deal in trademarks and patents. My partners could help there if you'd like."

Barry asked, "Are they who you would recommend?"

"Yes. Can I bring in Mr. Pandolfi to meet you? He can explain what he does and doesn't do, so you could decide." We both agreed and Emory left to get him.

Fredo! Barry was going to meet Fredo. This was better than I hoped.

Emory ushered Pandolfi into the room and introduced him. "This is Mr. Sal Pandolfi. He is very well versed in patents and trademarks. Sal, you know Mr. Handler. This is Mr. Myers, who is a teaching partner of his. They have a great project that I'll fill you in later about, but for now, they have a question about trademarks and patents."

"Be happy to help," Sal said.

Barry said, "This is a new teaching method for middle school that we wanted to protect and needed to have a framework of the process."

"Well. Have you applied for a trademark yet?"

"No."

"That's the first step and I see you have lots of material describing the program. I can help you do that and avoid some of the pitfalls that are sometimes in your way.

"Some elements of the program might not qualify if they are already in the public domain, but certainly it can be done and not very expensive to do, either. As your program grows, you might find your needs growing as well. The more popular it becomes, the more cautious and proactive you need to be about protecting your product."

"Can you do that as well?" we asked.

"We can. We also have worked with some bigger firms with more manpower if needed."

"Thanks. Thanks so much," Barry said.

Sal stood. "Any more questions for now?"

We both looked at each other and shook our heads.

Sal continued, "Well in that case, I look forward to

working with you in the future if we can help."

As he exited, Emory said, "I can remain as your point person if you'd like and handle everything you need. That way you're not making dozens of calls."

"Emory," I asked. "Could you do this right away if we go with you? I know some of what we ask might be a stretch."

"I can do it with my partners' backing, if that's acceptable. Very similar to ... um ..." Emory suddenly stopped and looked at me.

"It's okay, Emory, Barry knows all about our past involvement."

"Okay, good. Well then it's very similar to the time I represented you, Alan." After a short period of silence, Emory asked, "Do you guys have any other questions?"

I looked at Barry and he seemed very confident in Emory. I said, "Emory, thanks so much for sitting down with us. Barry and I will talk things over and get back in touch very soon."

Emory stood and shook hands with Barry and gave me another bear hug on the way out.

As we drove down the street I turned to Barry, "So what did you think?"

"Didn't you think that that Sal looked just like Fredo from The Godfather?"

I was stopped at the gate to St. Christopher's before I could get into the parking lot on Monday afternoon. A policeman came up to my window. "Sorry, sir. The school is closed today. Are you a teacher?"

I could see the parking lot ahead and there were a number of official-looking vehicles and media trucks parked near the entrance. "Yes. What's going on? ... I have a class today at 1 o'clock."

"All teachers are to report to the cafeteria for an announcement. You can go ahead."

I pulled into a parking spot and walked inside. My head was on a swivel. I was so new, I didn't even know where the cafeteria was yet. Mrs. Jones, the secretary for Father Kowolski, was standing at the doorway helping to direct traffic and to check for strays ... like me. She had been crying. I could tell by her face that there was something very sad happening here. She grabbed my arm. "Oh, good morning, Mr. Handler. If you would continue down this hall to the cafeteria. It's on your right. You'll see everyone there."

"What's going on, Mrs. Jones?"

"It's ... it's ... terrible ..."

The police sergeant came up to us about that time and asked if I could quickly move along for the announcement. I think I was the last to arrive. Mrs. Jones waved me on and said we would talk later.

The cafeteria was packed and many who were sitting there were already in tears. Reporters were milling around and setting up cameras along the walls. One of the nuns was standing at the podium with the sergeant on her right patiently waiting for everyone to get seated and quieted. "Good morning. If I could have your attention," she said, then paused once more and the room quieted. "I am sorry to report that this morning our beloved Father Stanley Kowolski was viciously attacked on his way to school." There were murmurs and sighs around the cafeteria, "Police Sergeant O'Malley will give more details and needs our help in finding the men who did this. Sergeant?"

"Thank you, Sister Marie. As the Sister said, Father Kowolski was beaten in his car apparently by three to four individuals. He was taken to Memorial Hospital in critical condition at about 9 this morning. Witnesses reported that at least one of those who were in on the attack had a St. Christophers uniform on. We will be here for a while longer interviewing anyone who might have information about the attack or the individuals that might have done it."

I couldn't believe what I was hearing. That wonderful priest who seemed like he wouldn't hurt a fly and loved his students was beaten in his car.

One of the reporters raised a hand. "Sergeant. Excuse me. Have you found out the motive yet?"

"No. Really don't know that yet. Although we do know that he had just made a withdrawal from the bank and the money was missing when we found him. There's a strong suspicion that robbery was at least one of the motives."

"You're saying that students were involved, correct?"

"Well, an eyewitness reported that there was at least one school uniformed attacker. The assumption was that it was a student."

Oh my God, I thought. I wonder if the money he withdrew was for the tuition he was covering for the students in our program. How horribly ironic. It makes this crime even more barbaric.

One of the policemen came up to the sergeant and whispered something. The sergeant then spoke on the mic. "I am so sorry to report that Father Kowolski has just passed away. His surviving sister and her family were by his side."

There were sobs and gasps heard after the announcement.

Sister Marie came to the microphone. "Father Mike will

say Mass immediately following this. All are invited to join us in prayer as we pray for our beloved Father Kowolski. May God have mercy on his beautiful soul."

There was chaos at the school when I finally left the campus. Classes were cancelled until Wednesday while police wrapped up the case and my course was cancelled indefinitely. I can't describe the feeling of sadness I felt that day. Although I only spent less than an hour with him, Father Kowolski had a profound impact on my life. And the student or students who literally murdered him were beyond contemptible.

Gary, Indiana was an even sadder place that morning.

I called Tommy Thompson the next day to give him the news. He had been following the media reports. It quickly became a national story.

"Sit tight, Alan. I have something else for you that is just finalizing and I think you'll be perfect for it."

I was starting to feel like an albatross in Indiana. I would be happy to get out of there. Other than the great association I had with Barry Myers, my arrest and the death of the school priest didn't bode well for my Indiana career.

Sitting there in my double-wide, I stared at the phone after hanging up with Thompson. Maybe I should try to call Karol. I was missing her terribly, craziness and all. I picked up the receiver and realized as I started to dial that I had no number for her. I had NO number for her. I didn't know her mother's number, a home number, I knew nothing.

I remembered her name was Sarah or Sara and she lived in Meridian. I tried the information operator but had no luck. There was one Ballard in Meridian, Roscoe Ballard. No relation.

Unlisted. It must be unlisted. I know. I'll call Thompson back. "Hey, Mr. T, I have a favor to ask. Do you have a number for Karol?"

"You don't have it?"

"I had it, but I just misplaced it, I guess."

Thompson had me hold while he checked the files.

"Have one that was in her files. It's a local number while she was here I guess. 504-555-1578."

"Thanks."

I called the number but there was a message, "I'm sorry. That number has been disconnected. If you have dialed this in error, please hang up and try again." It had been disconnected. Must have been one that she had before we hooked up.

I lay my head down on the pillow. Her pillow ... the phone was off the hook and making that irritating sound that phones make when they aren't hung up correctly. I didn't care. I just let it go to the floor as I closed my eyes and trailed off.

She really was gone.

The alarm went off at 7:30.

I reached over and hit the button, bleary-eyed and still half comatose from the night before. I was still in my clothes from yesterday and the phone was talking to me from the floor. "Please hang up the receiver to reconnect service ..." I sat up in bed and looked around. My mind was mush. So much had happened in such a relatively short time that I was having a hard time processing it all.

The phone rang.

"Alan," It was Thompson's voice on the other end. "Are you sitting down?"

"Uh, yeah as a matter of fact I am."

"Good, because I've got news that will knock you off your feet."

"Good news, I hope. I don't think I can take any more bad news."

"All good!" Thompson paused for dramatic emphasis. "You, my friend, are the newest overseas representative for READInc."

"I'm what?" At first I thought he said I'm the first over easy representative, whatever that meant.

"You are going overseas!"

"Wait. WHAT? As in Europe?"

"Bingo. Alan, we finalized the agreements and there are two programs that are starting back to back. One in Vienna, Austria and the other in Rome, Italy. And you're teaching both."

I was totally speechless.

"Did you hear what I said?" Thompson started to repeat it.

"No. I mean YES. YES. I heard you. I can't believe it. When do I go?"

"Immediately. That's how you got this assignment. You're the guy who has the time on his schedule right now."

More irony than I knew how to deal with. In the midst of total chaos in my life with things falling in every direction, this happens at the perfect time and it happens to of all people – me.

"Mr. T, thank you so much. Really. This means the world to me." I laughed at the words I used ... more irony. "Literally!"

CHAPTER FIVE

Stuck in a Fellini Movie

I felt the stress just slowly fall off my shoulders, as I flew through the clouds en route to Vienna.

It took a few days to get everything done. I finalized the double-wide rental payout, forfeiting the last month deposit due to terminating it early (it helped that I was getting a small raise and a supplemental paycheck from READInc in my new role). I visited Uncle Benny to return the car he generously got for me, thanking him profusely. I sent a small contribution to St. Christopher's in Father Kowolski's name with a note to Sister Marie telling her how truly sad I was about his death.

Barry and Isabel took me out for dinner to celebrate the new job. We talked at length about Community and our next steps. Barry and I had finalized things with Emory, who offered to start the project gratis and grow with us as he moved along in his career. Barry said that the kids were getting more motivated by the day. But some of the parents were a little less motivated to completely buy in .

"Get this," Barry said. "The other day Mr. George Ballantine calls me about his son, Danny, a seventh-grader in my class. He starts in on me about Danny's job in the community. Danny picked the lawyer position, right? So Mr. Ballantine IS a lawyer and says, 'Hey, I hear that Danny's salary is $10,000. I think that's foolish. He should get paid more'. Can you believe that? He wanted me to give Danny a raise."

"He complained that his son needed more fake money for his fake job?"

"Yeah. That's exactly right. So I told him that Danny did the research about income for attorneys in small town America and came up with a reasonable answer. He, of course, didn't agree."

"That's awful."

"That's exactly how I felt in the beginning. But really, the more I thought about it, it's kind of wonderful that the parents are now getting interested in our program as well. Even if it's to disagree. I think it's gonna pay off one day."

I saw Barry's point. When and if we marketed this program, parents needed to understand what we were doing for their kids and it's gonna be rocky at times. But better to have them involved than not. Barry was always thinking a step ahead. He had told me that maybe he could introduce a unit in Community where there was a role for parents working WITH their kids.

Isabel toasted to my future: "To the man who brought a little sunshine to Indiana, gave my husband renewed motivation in the classroom ..."

Barry completed the toast. "... and has decided to now leave us and become the ugly American in Europe."

"Hear, hear!" I added.

Delta Flight 234 touched down in Vienna just before noon. There was a lot for me to do before my classes started. Because I was the solo rep for READInc in Europe, I had to handle all the front work, test all the eligible students and really market the course. I also handled all the tuition payments and questions that the parents might have.

My course in Vienna really started after I finished up in Rome, but I needed to meet with the administration in Vienna first to get the ball rolling and introduce myself. The American International School network of independent schools worldwide was quite the prestigious group. Every major city (Paris, London, Hong Kong) had one. All of the American International Schools shared a common international holding company partner, 50% of the students were American and the prerequisite was that all students spoke English. The schools were filled with the kids of diplomats, business leaders and high-ranking military officers.

AIS in Vienna was located adjacent to the Vienna woods. You could see the Alps in the background and the city of Vienna in the foreground. The seven buildings that made up the campus were built along the ridge. It was like being transported to a fairytale land. So beautiful.

The head of school was William Neil. He had been there for over 20 years and was one of the senior leaders in the AIS network. He looked more like a diplomat than a head of school. When I first met Mr. Neil, I was totally intimidated. I was not only new to READInc but also new to the field of education and like a fish out of water in Vienna and here I was in one of the most prestigious schools in the world. Apparently READInc higher ups had faith in me and I didn't want to let anyone down.

"So, Mr. Handler. Where are are you from?" Mr. Neil peered over his half glasses as I sat in his office, which by the way was not overly ornate or large. It was very comfortable and ... normal.

"I was born in New Orleans, sir."

"Great place. Ever eat at Central Grocery on Decatur?"

"Sure! Home of the muffaletta." What the heck? Old Bill Neil was talking like a native. I couldn't picture him in CG eating a muff, but who knew?

"Mmmm. I can just taste it now." He sat back and savored the thought. "Years ago, I was teaching at Tulane University and that was my favorite place to go. The smells and sounds." He was definitely there.

"How about you? Where were you born, Mr. Neil?"

"Boston. Lived there most of my life."

"Beautiful city."

"Not my neighborhood. But I wouldn't have traded it for the world."

I was trying to figure him out. I guess my expression gave me away.

"You're wondering how a stuffy old fart like me came from that background, right?"

"Oh no, sir." He stared at me and grinned. "Well, I was kind of thinking that you looked so ... different ... from your past lives."

He got up and walked around his desk and took down a picture from his wall. It was an old family photo taken in front of a small tenement. Looked to be about 50 years old.

"This is my family. I look at them every day. My dad was a longshoreman and picked up extra work as a dishwasher and whatever else he could find to keep the family going. He sent every one of us to college and literally died doing it. But my mom always said he died a happy man because he was so proud of his kids." He placed the picture back and stared at it for a minute. "Never forget where you came from."

"That's inspirational, Mr. Neil."

"Ahhh, just real life. And now? Well, now I'm just an old stuffy fart pushing 70." He smiled. "Hey, Thompson told me about you, my boy, and I am really looking forward to having you join our staff when you get back from ... Rome, is it?"

"Yes, sir. I'm headed there now to start the course and should wrap it up in six weeks."

"Works for me." Bill Neil, my newest hero, stood and gave me a warm handshake and sent me on my way.

The train from Vienna to Rome left at 8 p.m.. Actually, at 8:03 p.m. on the dot. I learned quickly that Austrians were sticklers with details and schedules. The travel time was 13 hours and 23 minutes and I figured we would pull in precisely at 9:26 a.m..

I settled into my seat after arranging my two big suitcases the best I could. One bag had all my worldly possessions and the other had all my materials from READInc, like books and equipment and test booklets. The seats did not seem to recline, so sleeping would be a challenge. When the conductor came by to punch my ticket, I asked him, "Excuse me. Is there a way to recline these seats?"

"Sorry, no. But we do have sleeping cars that are available directly ahead."

"Do I need another ticket?"

"No ... I will warn you though. Those couchettes are small and there would be no place for your luggage. So, if I were you, I would leave your luggage here and come back when you awake."

I thanked him, tried to secure my luggage on my seat the best I could and walked to the sleeping car. Once inside, I saw what he was talking about. The couchettes were lining the sides of the train and were ... in effect ... cushioned recliner boards, not very comfortable but better than sitting up all night. There was no room for any baggage. I found an empty one, climbed up on it and closed the curtain.

The sound of the train and the vibration from the tracks put me right to sleep.

I woke up at about 8 a.m. amid lots of noise and activity outside the sleeping cars. Hopping out of my couchette, I put on my shoes and walked through the sleeping car toward my seat in the regular cabin.

Something was different.

I didn't recognize my seat. I checked my ticket and the seat I left the night before was still there but my luggage wasn't. That's what was different.

"Sir?" I said to a conductor who walked by. "I have a question." He stopped. "My baggage is missing. It was right here last night and now it isn't."

He looked at me quizzically and said something in Italian waving his arms above his head and walked off.

"Wait. Wait. My luggage. Have you seen my luggage?" He was gone.

Conductor number two entered and I also stopped him. "Sir. My luggage is gone. Can you help me?"

FOR THOSE WHO CAN

"Luggage?" He made it sound like I said Lu-gaj with his Italian accent. "No capisco."

"Does anyone speak English?" No one offered a hand. The conductor started to leave and then a smallish older gentleman stepped forward. "Do you speak English?" I asked desperately

"A little bit." He said.

"Would you tell the conductor my luggage was here last night and now it is gone. Can he help me?"

The little man translated and waited for an answer.

In Italian, the conductor said (via translator). "No one was here this morning in this seat. Someone complained that the luggage was in their way ... so we threw it off the train."

"WHAT? Why would you throw it off the train? I was told to sleep in the sleeping car and leave my luggage here until morning."

The Italian conductor asked, "Who told you that?"

"The conductor!"

"Ahhh ... the Austrian conductor. What does he know?"

I was dumbfounded. The little old man tried to help. He explained that we crossed the border between Austria and Italy a few hours ago. "That's where the Italian conductors take over from the Austrians. They apparently have different rules."

"So what do I do NOW?"

"Dogana. Dogana Roma." The Italian conductor waved his arms as if he gave up and stormed out.

"That's the Customs Office in Rome in the train station. He said that's who handles it now," the little old man said.

"I can't believe this. My luggage is somewhere in some town because someone just said they didn't want it there. I'm living a nightmare." I looked around for sympathy, but the rest of the passengers were just reading their newspapers and totally ignoring me.

I was in a new world now. Austrians were strictly by the book, very punctual and very practical. Italians seemed to be … off the grid!

In the train station I made a beeline to the Dogana. Inside, there were dozens of little desk tables manned by soldiers with the same uniform but different hats. Some had a plume and some had a feather and some were plain, but all were different.

I basically picked one at random since no one was looking like they wanted to help me.

"Do you speak English?" I asked the plume guy who looked the most important.

"A leeetle. Talk to Paolo. There."

Paolo was a plain hat guy. Great. Oh well. Here goes. "Paolo, do you speak English?"

"Yes I do. I am, how you say, fluente!" Paolo puffed out his chest.

"Good. Good. So Paolo I was on the train from Vienna and the conductor threw my luggage off the train when I was sleeping. Can you help me?"

"You have your passport?"

"Yes." I showed him my passport and he stamped it then wrote down my name.

"So you say he threw your bags off somewhere … right?"

"Right."

"You know where?"

"No."

"Hmmmm. But you sure he threw them off right?"

"Yes."

"Why he do that?"

"I don't know why he do that … did that. He said someone complained they were in his way." GEEZ!

"Okay. Here's what happen now. I send a message to all towns along the route. I ask who got your baggage. The one who does I tell to send it here. Okay?"

"Okay. Good. How long does that take?"

"Well. They should get the message in about a week."

"A week? It takes a week?"

"Ah, you know. Some of them don't open their mail and some are not there certain days … so that's how you say … an estimate. Then whoever got them should send them."

"So a week right?"

"For the bags to get here? Oh no. I would say another week or so at least."

"Two weeks, then? Two weeks?"

"You check in every few days and I give you a dateline."

"Dateline?"

"Yes, you know, tell you what I found out."

"Oh, an update. You'll give me an update."

"Good." He looked at me sympathetically as I stood there looking around wondering where I go now. "Hey, you have a place to stay in Roma, my friend?"

"Not yet."

"My brother has pensione off the Via Veneto. It is very nice and clean. Here is his address," He wrote it down. "I put my name here too ... if you're interested."

"Thanks ... thanks so much."

I grabbed a cab and sat back, empty-handed. I was carrying travelers checks and a credit card. Thank God I didn't pack them. But what about clothes? And all my teaching supplies?

I started to make lists in my mind ... Call READInc and tell them what happened, buy clothes, visit the school and talk to the administration, and spend time at the train station EVERY DAY.

The taxi pulled up to the address that I gave him. I really didn't know what the heck a pensione was, so I didn't expect much.

This was somebody's home.

I walked up to the front door and rang the bell.

"Si?"

"Hi, I hope you speak English. I'm looking for Signore Capaletti."

"Si. I am Capaletti."

"My name is Alan Handler. Your brother Paolo said you might have a pensione available?"

"Si. Si. Come in, Mr. Handler."

He ushered me in and led me to a room off the central hallway. I have to say, I was blown away. It was beautiful. Hand-painted frescos on the ceiling, four poster bed, very elegant place. "This room has a WC and a shower over there.

And of course it includes dinner with my family. How long would you wanta the place?"

I was holding my breath to hear the price. "At least a month. Can you rent it by the month."

"Oh yes. That is no problema." He calculated. "That would be 320,000 lira."

I gasped. "What is that in ... dollars?"

He calculated. "Is about $250."

"Oh, that is fine. I'll take it." I was so relieved. He could have said anything lower than $320,000 and I would have said fine.

"You have luggage?"

"No." I paused. "I'm waiting for that to arrive."

"Good. Let's do paperwork, okay?"

He introduced me to his wife Sophia and his son Giovanni, who were in the kitchen. All spoke English and made me feel welcomed. He also showed me to their phone and told me I could make calls from there and he would just charge my room.

I was so grateful for a place to use as a base while I got my head together.

Thompson was my first call. He was concerned. "Alan, what are you gonna do? How long do you think it will take to get your stuff."

"According to Dogana in Rome ... anywhere from two weeks to 35 years."

"No, seriously."

"I wish I was kidding. I have no idea. Listen, I plan to buy some clothes to get me by. Can you send me some reading materials?"

"Yes. I can do that. Do you need copies of the rosters and the school info?"

"I do. And listen, Tom, can you give me an advance? I promise I'll repay."

"Let me see what I can do to help out there. I'm sure we can do that."

"I'm not sure how much I have on my credit card but I'll use it until I can't anymore."

"Hang in there, buddy."

"Trying to."

Giovanni Capaletti was close to my age. We bonded immediately. Actually, I bonded with the whole Capaletti family immediately. Sophia and Vito were the salt of the earth. Eating dinner with the family was extra special. They rented out only the one bedroom so it was literally like being the second son, and Sophia's cooking was to die for.

Every Monday night they watched movies on television together. Many were old American movies and I got the biggest kick watching Humphrey Bogart speaking Italian.

Gio offered to take me shopping when he heard my situation. We walked down the Via Veneto to a little shop that was tucked away in one corner. He introduced me to the owner and told him I needed the works. "Well," I said, "that depends on what the works cost ... maybe I'll do the 'almost' works."

I quickly found out that Italian clothes were made for skinny guys with no butts who liked everything tight. That was definitely not my style nor my physique. After trying on

FOR THOSE WHO CAN

all the wrong clothes, I finally asked, "Do you have anything in a boys' husky?"

The owner laughed and took me into the back room where he had another selection of clothes for what he called the "well-developed man." I knew it as "the fat room." It worked out well.

I managed a suit, a couple pairs of slacks and a few shirts that I could wash regularly, a pair of shoes, socks and underwear, and a couple of ties. It stretched my budget some, but I didn't know when, if ever, I would see my baggage again.

I had the same mix of apprehension and excitement that I felt in Vienna when I saw my new school. Marymount International School of Rome was an incredible place. I had read that Marymount was part of a Catholic chain of prestigious international schools in Europe, South America and the U.S. It was private, coed and managed by Dutch nuns who did not wear the traditional habits and lived more secular lives. When the taxi pulled in, I was struck by the size of the campus, which covered 40 acres and looked more like a villa than a school. In fact, as I found out, when the sisters moved to this location in the early 50s, it WAS a villa. They added a few buildings, classrooms and dorms, to accommodate a growing population.

My course was set to start in exactly one week.

"Sister Margaret. It's a pleasure meeting you," I said as I entered the office of Sister Margaret, the head of school, a very pleasant woman who was gracious and had an air of elegance and compassion.

"Mr. Handler, very nice to meet you as well. I'd like to

introduce you to Shannon Gallagher. She is our reading specialist here at Marymount and I thought it might be good for her to sit with you before your course starts." I didn't see Shannon right away when I walked in. She was standing by Sister Margaret's bookshelves on the far wall.

"I think that's great. Do I call you Sister as well?"

"No. Just Shannon would be fine. I am a secular teacher. Nice to meet you, Mr. Handler. I am thrilled to have you here."

I paused as we all sat. "I should tell you that there were some problems getting here but I think all will be fine."

"Oh no," Sister Margaret said. "Is everything okay?"

"Mostly, yes. On the train from Vienna, my luggage was mistakenly removed in the middle of the night while I was sleeping, but Customs is working to get them back for me."

"How on earth did that happen?"

"Still struggling with that answer, Sister." I turned to Shannon. "One bag had all my teaching supplies like readers and equipment. READInc is sending more but in case that's delayed, are there materials that I could borrow?"

"Certainly, Mr. Handler. I would be happy to help."

"That's a relief. I'm sure I won't need much to supplement once I get the materials from home."

Sister Margaret stood. "Well, I have a class starting in just a few minutes. Shannon, would you be so kind as to show Mr. Handler around?"

"Certainly."

I shook Sister Margaret's hand and told her how happy I was to be there. Shannon then escorted me to the cafeteria. A group of students who were finishing lunch waved to Shannon. One called out, "Hi, Miss Gallagher."

"Hi, Sally. Hello, girls." They walked to our table. "This is Mr. Handler. He will be joining us for a couple of months to teach a course in study skills and college prep."

"That's cool," Sally said. "Nice to meet you."

"You too, Sally."

As they left, I returned to Shannon and asked her about the student population. She told me that there were two dormitories for the girls. They made up the majority of the population of the school but there were day students as well, many of them boys. Everyone spoke English and more than half were American and British ... very similar to Vienna.

"So how long have you been here, Shannon Gallagher?" I asked.

"Well, I went to school here way back in ancient times. I left for the states and graduated from Columbia with an Education degree and then came back. It's been three years now."

"You must really like it."

"I love it. When you walk the campus, meet the students and join the faculty. I bet you'll feel the same way."

Shannon was a natural beauty. She had bright Irish eyes, reddish hair that hung in tight curls to her shoulders and an athletic figure.

"Your family lives here?"

"Daddy works at the American Embassy as a Public Health Specialist." She stopped and looked at me. "Did I just say 'Daddy' out loud?"

"You did."

"Embarrassing,"

"He's NOT your Daddy?"

"No. I mean, yes he is my DAD. I sound like a little twit saying 'Daddy,' don't I?"

"No. Not at all. Now ... what about your Mommy, your Nanny, your PopPop and your BooBoo?" I smiled, hoping she had a sense of humor.

She howled. "We all live in a Gingerbread House at the end of Jellybean Alley and bake muffins all day."

"Now that would be something to see."

Shannon stood, "For starters, I'll give you the official Shannon Gallagher 50 cent tour of Marymount."

"I'd like that." And I truly did.

"So ... this place is awesome." I had placed a call to Barry Myers right before we sat down to dinner. I couldn't stop talking about the school. They had everything. New labs and equipment, big classroom space, large soccer and practice fields. "Barry, for a history teacher it's paradise. The city, the architecture, the culture ..."

"Did you ever get your bags?"

"You had to ruin it, huh? NO. This place sucks."

"Make up your mind."

"I talked to my new best friend, Paolo, in the Dogana Office and he had no news, No one stepped up so he knows nothing about where it is."

"What are you gonna do?" he whispered into the phone.

"Well, Gio, my new brother here, knows a guy who knows a guy who knows a guy ... and he said that for the right price they can help me out."

"Sounds kinda sketchy."

"Ya think? Yeah I'm a-gonna give-a my buddy Paolo a few more days and see what happens."

"Good luck."

"Seriously, Barry. I wish you could maybe take a year and teach overseas and see these schools. Vienna seems pretty cool too."

"You do know I have two kids."

"Probably not really practical right now huh?"

"Well, maybe when Community hits the educational market and we make our first mil and I take a lonnnng vacation."

"How's it going by the way?"

"You remember the idea we talked about ... adding a marriage component?"

"Yeah ... planning for a wedding, then putting together a joint budget, planning for a family and stuff?" (Sophia called me to dinner and I motioned to Sophia that I would be just another minute.) "That was a good idea."

"I thought so. We had one taker and now they want a divorce."

"Ha ha. Hey it's not that attorney's kid is it ... the one who wanted a raise."

"No, thank God."

"Well ... it IS real life stuff."

"A little too real."

After dinner, Gio and I walked to a little cafe on the Via Venetto and sat outside under the stars. We had cappuccinos and talked about America. Gio wanted to know everything about our culture and politics and as I was answering his questions, I realized how little I really knew about my own country. He had a friend who lived in New Hampshire and wanted to know all about the state. I knew how to spell it. He asked me about the Boston Tea Party because he saw it in a movie. I knew they threw tea overboard.

I had taken history for granted. History is everything in Europe. They had a long extensive history and ours has been short in comparison. But if you were to ask Gio about details about the various wars in and around Italy, the churches of Rome and the artists who created masterpieces there, he would know. Considering their history is centuries old and ours is measured in decades, I was truly embarrassed and impressed at the same time.

Every few minutes a gorgeous woman would walk by. There is no shortage of gorgeous women on the Via Veneto. Before I could say, "Gio, check her out," she would wave or wink at Gio and tell him hello.

"Do you know them all, Gio?"

"Hey ... I grew up in this neighborhood. I know lots of people."

"So far the females seem to be the ones that know you best."

Just then a group of three knockouts came up to our table and kissed and hugged Gio while I sat with my mouth open. "Sit. Sit, ladies," Gio said to them. YES ... I thought. Sit, ladies. "This is my friend Alan. Alan, this is Gina, Maria and Angela." I reached across to shake their hands and spilled coffee in my lap.

"Oooo poor thing. Let me help." Gina or Maria or Angela jumped up and grabbed a napkin and dabbed it all around my lap to blot the coffee.

Gio had a big grin on his face. I was living the dream!

I arrived at Dogana first thing in the morning, as I had every morning for the past two weeks. "Where is Paolo?" I asked a Dogana official.

"Passport?"

I handed it to him and he stamped it again. My passport was now covered with stamps – meaningless, inked stamps – that I got every time I came. I think that is the only thing these guys do. They certainly don't find lost baggage.

"Is Paolo here?"

"No. Paolo on vacation." The officer said with his head down, in stamping some documents (of course).

"When will he be back?"

The officer stopped and looked up at me obviously annoyed. "Can we help you with something?"

"My bags have been lost and Paolo was trying to get them returned. Did you get any returned bags?"

"I will check." He walked to another desk and picked up a notebook. He scanned the first few sheets. I noticed his English was very good. I was pretty sure that all these guys could speak perfect English. They were just selective at times. "No, signore. Nothing for a Mr. Handler."

"I'll check tomorrow. Thanks."

Crazy, I thought as I walked through the terminal. Just crazy. I spotted a conductor taking a break on one of the benches and stopped to sit. "I'm sorry to bother you, but can I ask a question?"

"Si?"

I told him my story without asking if he spoke English. I just hoped he did after all of that. "Is there any other recourse I have instead of waiting for Dogana to act?"

"Oh, signore. I understand. You see, our Dogana is trying hard, but there are not enough people to keep up, you know?"

"Yes. I understand. But what do I do?"

He looked around like a man about to tell me a secret and motioned for me to sit closer. "I can help."

"You can?"

"Yes. You see the conductor across from us by the counter?"

"I do."

"He does that route twice a week." He looks at his watch. "I will talk to him. He can check at each stop for your baggage and when he finds it, he can put it on board and bring it back here."

"If he can do that it would be great!" I said.

"Okay. Well, he will need some money for the men who handle baggage."

I reached in my pocket on instinct. "How much?"

"I think … 2000 lira should do it."

"Okay," I counted out 2000 lira and handed it to him.

"Wait here and I'll get an answer."

He strode over to the counter and talked to the other conductor. He pointed in my direction and they both did the Italian waving of hands as they talked and he came back. "He will do it."

"Good."

"But he needs another 1000 lira to make it work, he said."

I slowly took out the remaining lira I had in my pocket. "I only have 500 lira left."

He grabbed it. "That should do. He was, how you say, estimating."

I was skeptical but he assured me, saying. "Not to worry. We will get it done, my friend." We shook hands and he made his way back over to the other conductor. They talked some more and as I got up to leave, they looked over and laughed and split the money between them.

I was never going to see that money or my baggage in his hands again, that's for sure.

Believe it or not, a week later, I got a call at the Pensione from Paolo. "Mr. Handler. Your two bags are here at the station. You can pick them up in the Dogana."

"Wow! That's great news, Paolo. Thank you so much."

"No problem. Sorry it took a while but one of our baggage men called a few days ago and spotted them in a corner of his station." I figured that the slimy bastard that took my 2500 lira had nothing to do with it. He had pretended not to know me after that, anyway.

When I got to the Dogana the next day, Paolo was working a later shift so another officer took me into the giant warehouse where there were hundreds of bags sitting along the walls and stacked in corners. There was a huge amount of dust on many of them. I was relieved mine was not in one of those corners. He spotted my bags and carried them to a large table so I could check them.

"This one is mine," I pointed to a familiar bag. "But the other is not."

"Si." The officer started to take both bags back."

"Wait. That one is mine."

"SI?" He held them up. He spoke no English. I pointed to the one and nodded and said no to the other.

He was disgusted and again turned to put them back.

"NO. NO. Sorry I am mistaken. I'll take them both!"

He stopped again and held them up and I nodded yes to both. I figured I would just take both and return the other to the rightful owner when I found out who it was. Otherwise, I might never see either again. The missing suitcase had my READInc supplies and they had been replaced by Tommy Thompson earlier in the week.

"Passport?" He said, "Of course," and I handed it to him. This time, he stamped it and pointed to the next table. The man at that table looked at the paperwork and stamped it again. Then he pointed and the next man stamped it as well. This continued for three more tables. In the end, I finally took the suitcases to the pensione.

I realized that day that Fellini movies were in fact not dreamlike, surreal ravings. They were honest depictions of REAL LIFE in Italy.

The suitcase that was not mine had a layer of dust on it that I carefully wiped down before I laid it on my bed to see who it belonged to. It opened easily and was neatly packed.

It belonged to a man. His clothes were folded and covered something beneath. When I lifted them out I saw an old Nikon camera. He must be a collector, I thought because it was at least 20 years old. Under that was a folder with slides, presentation slides that are shown in a projector. These were glass slides, which I thought were interesting, as well because glass slides weren't used for some time. There was an unused rail ticket that I opened which had his name, Captain Howard Malden. And ... Holy crap ... the ticket was dated March 21, 1956. This bag has been sitting for twenty years.

I looked closely at the slides. They were medical procedure slides. Heart and lungs and other organs. I searched more and found some correspondence. Captain Malden was affiliated with Walter Reed Hospital. He was a heart surgeon and undoubtedly looked for this bag for a long time. I found his phone number, neatly labeled inside his slide folder. I called it immediately.

He answered.

He thanked me profusely, told me that they disappeared in Rome years ago when he was speaking at a conference and he had just given up hope. He was most excited about his camera. I told him everything was intact.

The next day, two marines came to the pensione to collect the bag. They brought a nice gift of cheeses and chocolates and a note of thanks from the grateful doctor.

I smiled to myself and thought I wonder if 20 years from now, someone opens my READInc bag and has the same thought.

My course in Rome was going well. Shannon had been wonderful to work with and had shared many of her reading books that gave extra dimension to my program.

She and I spent lots of time together sightseeing. She was a wealth of information about Roman history and knew something about every church – well, not all of them. After all, there are over 900 churches in Rome and two thirds of those are Catholic. She knew the major players.

I have to admit: I was attracted to Shannon. She was so genuine and so humble. She was also unaware of her beauty. If she was aware, she fooled me. You would never know it by her actions. No makeup, no frills.

I was still holding onto a broken heart that Karol did a number on. I knew that I would probably never hear from her, but I couldn't shake her. I hadn't heard from her since she left and couldn't find out where she was. Probably a good thing. I would probably stand outside her door and look pathetic.

I think Shannon had a crush on me. Actually, I know she did. One of the other teachers kept asking me when I was going to ask Shannon out on a real date. I avoided that question as often as I could until Shannon asked me herself.

"So?" We were eating gelato on the steps of a small out of the way church when she suddenly turned to me and asked the question. "Is this a real date?"

"Um, let's see. This was a planned outing between a boy and a girl. I asked you and now we are having something to eat. Yeah. Yeah, this is a real date."

"And you don't feel pressure, do you?"

"How so?"

"Expectations."

"Not until you asked me if this was a real date."

I scooted closer. "Hey. We never really talked about real dates before, but I told you all about my convoluted feelings about Karol."

"I'm not talking about a marriage proposal, Alan. Just a date."

"I know. I'm sorry Shannon. I just …"

"I get it. Just forget I even said anything. I have no expectations. I just wanted to know your feelings about … you know … us."

"Shannon, you are wonderful. Seriously. I feel so normal and happy with you."

"Me too," she said and leaned over to kiss me. It was square on the lips but without the passion of a romantic kiss but the warmth of something more.

I used READInc as my forwarded address since I started the job. Mail from Camden and from South Bend and even my old address in New Orleans was forwarded there. Every so often I would get a personal letter from a friend or a teacher or even a student.

I was always excited to get mail from home. A few days after my "real date" with Shannon I got a real letter from Karol. I didn't see it right away. It was mixed in with letters from Barry Myers, Emory and a cute letter from Candace telling me that she was accepted by Howard University and was on her way to the first step in her quest to be a veterinarian. Barry told me I'd be hearing from Emory with more paperwork and Emory had sent it to me.

Then I saw Karol's letter.

I was shocked. It was totally unexpected, of course. The postmark was from Meridian and the return address was a P.O. box. I closed my door and carefully opened it as if it would self destruct if I rushed it. I read it three times:

Dearest Handler

I promised myself I wouldn't do this. I was moving on and not looking back. It worked for a while but I really hated not being able to talk to you. This is the next best thing for me. I want to hear all about you and what you are doing. I miss you. But I understand if you don't want to write back.

Living with me had to drive you nuts. If it's any consolation, living with me drives me nuts too. I'm in Mississippi with my family. I get my mail from a post office box. I think it's best if we don't exchange addresses. I can send stuff to READInc.

In time ... you will understand why I chose this way. I want you to know that it is not and never has been because of the way I feel about you. You are still one of the most special people ever in my life. No one has been more patient, more loving and respectful than you, Handler. And no one has been more of a pain in the ass than me. I know that. I'm so lucky to have had you in my life.

Here's hoping we can continue!

Much Love

KRB

There was a knock at the door.

"Let's get drunk, Alan." It was Gio and it was perfect timing.

We sat in our favorite cafe, saw our favorite women and got a visit from our favorite hotties.

"She wrote to me," I said as Gio was smothered by the three beauties.

"Who wrote you?"

"Karol. My girlfriend."

"The crazy one?"

I laughed. "Yeah, the crazy one."

"So what kind of letter? Good one? Bad one?"

"It was a very good one."

"That's good, right? Why do you look like shit if it was good?"

"I don't know. I was just getting over her and now ..." One of the three beauties gave me a big kiss. I was never sure who was who. I think it was Gina.

"She likes you too, my friend."

"You so CUTE," Gina said and kissed me again. Then the three of them said goodbye and strutted down the street.

"Gio," I said, "I don't get it. You have these women coming up to you all the time. They all love you. What's the deal? All I have is one crazy one that writes me letters now but never wants to meet face-to -face again."

"Alan ... these girls all work for me."

"Huh?"

"They all work for me."

"What do they do?"

"Well ... they all work at night and bring me money and I buy them clothes that look very sexy. Can you figure it out?"

"Oh my God. You're a pimp. These are your girls. I get it!" I burst out laughing and sat in Gio's lap. "Can I be one of your girls, too?" I gave him a big kiss on the lips.

That night I came home more than a little buzzed but feeling energized. I wrote a note to Candace telling her how proud I was of her and wanted to hear from her when she got to Howard. I signed the formal agreement with Emory and wrote to Barry to do a virtual toast to our official partnership. I then wrote to Karol:

Dearest Karol

I like saying dearest to you almost as much as I like reading it from your letter.

I was more than thrilled to get your letter by the way. I'm not sure what hallucinogenic caused you to write to me but please take them again soon. Of course I will write. Yes. I have missed you too and yes I was very good to you and yes you are a royal pain in the ass but ... you are my pain in the ass and I kinda got used to the feeling.

I'm wrapping up my course in Rome (yes, Rome you would have LOVED it) and I head to Vienna in a few days to start another. If that entices you, I'll use it often.

Come to Vienna.

I promise that I'll play it your way and not put addresses or phone numbers and use READInc as my mailbox. I'll send you something every day so that you can maybe experience this great adventure with me.

By the way, Barry and I signed on with Emory to represent our new partnership "Community" and it's apparently doing great.

I hope you're well and you're happy. I really do.

I look forward to our next conversation.

Love you lots

Handler

Shannon and the staff threw me a wonderful party on my last day of class. They bought a beautiful book highlighting Catholic Churches in Rome and brought out a big cake that simply said "Goodbye and good luck Sr. Fellini" ... a reference to my constant whining about how wild Rome was. Shannon put together a little care package filled with tele-calling cards, emergency phone numbers, a get-out-of- jail-free card (If she only knew how true that was!) and a return ticket to Rome.

Shannon was the perfect girl. She just happened to have terrible taste in men. I was lucky to have known her.

The Capalettis made one more incredible dinner of ossobuco ala Milanese before I left. I bought them a few bottles of the best wine I could find and told them how much I appreciated everything. Gio and I took one more stroll around the Via Veneto. He tried to give me Gina for the night, which was very tempting, but I declined.

I told him he DEFINITELY was my hero.

FOR THOSE WHO CAN

CHAPTER SIX

Vienna Waits For You

*D*earest Karol

I got to Vienna today. Good news: I didn't lose my luggage! Got a cool little place to live. It's not too far from the school. I take the bus ... the 35A . You'd be proud. I pulled out my guitar and wrote a tune about it. Been a while since I did that huh? The lyrics go like this:

The 35A goes one way/Gets to the end and goes the other way/Comes back down/Turns around/Never gets to town never leaves the ground/The 35A's coming back again this way.

Silly little thing.

Well gotta run ... Love ya lots

Handler

My course at AIS started almost immediately. Bill Neil handed me off to the Reading Specialist, Susan Blackburn. It was interesting that the International schools like Rome and Vienna invested in reading specialists. I didn't see that in American schools, and it was paying off here. The students were light years ahead of their counterparts in the U.S.

Vienna was an interesting place. Because it was at the crossroads between Eastern Europe and Western Europe, some of the students were transitioning from countries that were very difficult and oppressive for families and consequently there was a little PTSD problem to contend with.

For example, two of my students were Jewish and came from Russia. They were emigrating to Israel and Vienna was their transitioning city. I saw a very frightened look in their eyes when they were sitting in class trying to understand the culture and to blend with the other students. At one point, there was an announcement over the loudspeaker and both students dove under their desks. They stayed there with their heads covered by their arms until I came over to tell them all was okay. I can only imagine what horrors they had to endure in their prior lives.

The contrasts were stunning.

Many of the students were attached to the various embassies in Vienna. These were impressive embassies where a great deal of high-level world talks took place. The U.S. Ambassador's son was in my class. On the first week of my classes, the Ambassador invited faculty from the school to the embassy for a little party. I remember walking through the place in awe. Everywhere I looked, there were faceplates that depicted some event or meeting that took place there. On one table there was a faceplate that read "Kennedy and Khrushchev dinner and discussions 10/61." On a chair there was "Vince Lombardi visit 5/59." It was like a museum of the rich and famous.

I met Karl Rosen at that party.

He was the kindergarten teacher and a real character himself. Karl and I became very close friends while I was there. He had unusual teaching methods, like filling the kindergarten library with books on everything from gardening to carpentry to art to plumbing. These were not children's books and it was Karl's theory that the earlier you got kids interested in reading words from books that they might find at home, the further ahead the kids will be.

His classroom was set up with VW bus benches and stuffed chairs. He would show old home movies to the kids and they would in turn use their imagination to create stories about what they saw. It was rare to have a man teach kindergarten and Karl was beloved by the students and teachers alike.

Karl introduced me to the big Flea Market in Vienna in the center of town. He went just about every Sunday to look for treasures. His favorites were train conductor watches and old brass irons that used hot bricks of varied shapes and sizes to iron clothes.

I told Karl about our Community idea, knowing that he would love it.

"Oh, man. Now that's something that should have wings and really take off. I could use it in Kindergarten, too."

"You could? How would it work?"

"Oh sure. People don't give younger kids enough credit. Town meetings would be super cool. The town problems might be different but could be in their terms like: We need volunteers to help deliver lunches to the elderly, or, let's draw maps for the people to find their way to town because the road is closed for repairs. Stuff like that."

"Pretty brilliant, Karl."

I called Barry. "So what foreign country have you invaded this week, Handler?"

"Austria."

"Cool, visit the house where Hitler grew up."

"Um … not on my list, buddy."

"So, did you call to brag about how great everything is again?"

"Yes," I said laughing. "And to tell you that I have another recruit to help with curriculum. The kindergarten teacher had great ideas on how to use it in lower school. He's gonna write some thoughts down, too." I shared our conversation and Barry was very interested.

"It's about time you pulled your weight. By the way, I presented at a national conference last week and there is lots of interest in the program. We still have a lot of work to do before we take this out to the public."

"I know. I have been zero help to you."

"Good thing is, we can make our own timeline. And since you have much more important things to do, I will just manage my poor struggling family while you trot around the globe."

"Bite me."

My course was sailing along as was my confidence level. The more I taught, the more comfortable I got with classroom teaching. The students also made it enjoyable and easy. They were among the brightest I've ever encountered and needed very little encouragement to prepare for the next level. They were there.

My comfort level was briefly shaken only once when I was teaching at AIS.

Two seniors, Becky and Amanda, stayed after class one day for some post grad advice. Apparently, they both had been accepted to Boston College and decided that they both wanted to study business.

"Mr. H," Becky started the conversation. "My father wants me to go to law school and I'm not sure I want to do that. Amanda and I have an idea that we think rocks."

"What's your idea?"

"Men's Grooming Salons," Amanda chimed in. "You know, staffed with young pretty girls who really take care of all men's needs." She winked.

As the blood rushed to my face, I'm sure Rudolph would have been jealous.

"Shaving, hair styling, facials, manicures … that kind of stuff." Becky added.

I relaxed a little. "Well, sounds like you've thought about this a lot and speaking as a man, I think it has a lot of merit. Our barber shops are pretty boring. Adding some of the same amenities that women have in their salons is a good idea."

"So you'd support our idea?" They were both sitting across from me and I noticed that Becky had a few buttons undone on her top and was leaning forward and Amanda had hiked up her short skirt and had uncrossed her legs.

Rudolph was back! "Well … um … yes I think it sounds like a good idea."

"Good," Becky continued. "We want to tell our parents that we got solid teacher support on this. Can they call you?"

"Wait. Wait. I didn't say that you should necessarily do this. Law school is always a great option and maybe you could do that first and see after that."

"Aw, please, Mr. Handler. Please help us out." They both were now standing and had me cornered in the room. I mean literally cornered. I grabbed my books from the desk and held them in front of me looking toward the door and praying that no one would come in.

The next thing that happened was a blur. I think it was Amanda who reached under my books and grabbed my crotch. Becky also leaned in, "You are really our favorite teacher, you know?"

I took a deep breath and pushed them both out of the way, sounding like my mother, "Girls. This is really inappropriate!"

In my mind, I pretty much galloped out of the room.

Dearest Karol

My classes are going well. These students are so different from any of the others we taught. Much more mature and aggressive. A little intimidating at times but I guess it keeps life interesting.

We have a really tight group of teachers that somehow adopted me. Karl (who everybody calls Crazy Karl) the kindergarten teacher, Susan the Reading teacher and Marty who teaches third graders.

Weekends, we all take a trip somewhere together.

Got a Eurail pass, which is really cheap. Travel here between

countries is like going to nearby states. This weekend we are
going to Czechoslovakia. Hope I don't have to spell it.

Miss your face.

Write me!

Lots of love

Handler

It was no surprise to me that I hadn't heard from Karol since her first letter. I had hoped for more but in truth was blown away that she wrote me the first letter. It didn't really matter. Writing her every day was a way for me to journal this amazing wrinkle in time.

Prague in 1976 was a depressing place. We didn't see much when we were there. But what we did see was eye-opening for me. It was my first experience with Communism.

In 1968, The Socialist Republic of Czechoslovakia was going through a change. What became known as the Prague Spring when Alexander Dubcek was elected First Secretary, was the beginning of a new although short-lived era in Eastern Europe. Dubcek had tremendous support from the Czech citizens when he introduced sweeping reforms such as relaxation of censorship of the media, speech and travel. Czechoslovakian artists were flourishing at that point and many liberals were vehemently opposed to the Russian ideals and the Russian regime under Brezhnev.

However, in 1969, Russian tanks and military invaded Prague and within months, the spring was replaced by "normalization" back to the stringent communist limitation of rights. Dubcek was removed from office and a dark period fell over the country.

What we saw when we were there seven years after the invasion was a country of repressed citizens who were hard-pressed to make a living and unable to find a voice to help change it.

We arrived by bus and were stopped on the border. The military collected our passports and told us to remain on the bus while they checked our bags and carry-on items for propaganda like Time magazines, newspapers and any material that we carried that was deemed to be "unfit." They also warned us to stay within a certain district and that if any citizen asked to purchase any items from us, we needed to refuse. A popular item was bluejeans. A sale of your bluejeans could put both you and the buyer in jail.

I'm not sure how high on the dangerous-propaganda meter bluejeans were, but apparently it was high enough to create a category.

Once we were allowed to get off the bus, we stayed within a 10-square block area. That said, the Old Town Square was a striking example of wonderful architecture and brilliant mechanics.

On the Old Town Hall sat the Prague Astronomical Clock which has been there since 1410. It was the oldest working astronomical clock in the world. It had three main components: an astronomical dial which had the current position of the sun and the moon in the sky: statues of various Catholic saints on either side of the dial complete with the "walk of the apostles," which was an hourly show of moving saints and apostle figures striking the time; and a calendar dial with medallions representing months.

It was definitely worth the trip.

We sat for a cup of coffee in the square. Karl stared at the clock for a very long time and said – as only Karl would – "I wonder if I could build one of those clocks when I get back."

"You mean a replica, right?" Susan asked.

"No, I mean a big one like that." He pointed excitedly. "Can you imagine how excited the kids would be?"

Karl was dead serious. If he could have gotten his hands on materials to build something like that, as impractical as it sounds, he would try to build it. Crazy Karl was one of a kind.

On the walk back to the bus, I counted four people who offered me money for my jeans. I was afraid to look at Karl. He would have stripped them off right in the middle of the street just to test out the jeans policy.

Dearest Karol,

My course wraps up in a week and then summer vacation starts. I'm not sure what I want to do next. Thompson asked if I want to re-sign with READInc and come back to the states. I asked him what the possibility of working in Europe would be next year and he said there aren't any programs in the queue right now. Plenty in the states.

I think I want to stay a little longer over here ... at least over the summer. And actually, Bill Neil, the headmaster here, said he might have a position as a full time position next year for me.

Not sure what to do. Well, if you do decide to write soon I would love to get your thoughts.

Love ya

Handler

Crickets from Meridian.

Still no letters from Karol and no expectations from me. When I was in my apartment writing letter number 56 or 57 or 58, I felt foolish to keep holding on. I probably reread the only letter she wrote to me every time I wrote one to her and hung on those words "the most special person in my life" and "most loving."

On the days that I was the most hopeful, I imagined her writing me every day and filing them away or tearing them up so as to not create false hope. On darker days, I would imagine her going out with a new guy every day telling them all, "This guy in Vienna carries a torch and I love to just lead him on and keep him guessing."

Of the buddy group, the first to leave in the summer was Karl. He started a new job in Florida. It was a small private school in St. Petersburg. He would still teach kindergarten but would also serve as chair of their curriculum council and get a little higher salary to boot. He told me how much he loved the beach. A New Yorker all his life until he came to Vienna, Karl was ready for the beach life.

Marty and Susan were going to travel to Amsterdam and then to the states for a while to visit their folks in Connecticut and Wisconsin. They were planning to come back midsummer for some local travel. Marty came from a very wealthy family in Connecticut. In fact the small town they lived in carried the family name. Her great grandfather or great great grandfather built that town and made his fortune in the textile industry. Marty was the product of a stellar education holding a Masters degree from Smith and a PhD from Brandeis. I believe it was in sociology or psychology one; either way, she never used it in her career. She had told us that her family was very disappointed with her choice of careers. Her brother was a neurosurgeon in Boston and her sister was the CEO for one of the big three accounting firms in New York. Her mom always introduced her as an educational specialist for lower school curriculum in Vienna. She always countered with, "I teach third grade!" Very grounded.

Susan was from Madison, Wisconsin. Both her parents were educators. Both went to University of Wisconsin and both never left. Susan was the first to venture out. She was far from being a risk taker. Never married, Susan studied Library Sciences in school and was a proud introvert.

Before the buddy group headed out for the summer, we spent a long weekend together on a bike trip through the Austrian countryside. Karl took the lead pretty much the whole way as he sang "The hills are alive with the Sound of Music" until we all beat him senseless with our backpacks.

"We are not in Salzburg," I said.

"There are STILL hills, right?" Karl countered.

We stopped at a few family-owned vineyards and tasted their wines and picnicked by the Danube. None of us fully appreciated at that time how lucky we were to be able to enjoy all that beauty together. There was a popular book published that year that each of us carried ... *Europe on Five Dollars a Day*. And in 1976 in Austria sipping wine and eating bread and cheese feeling like we just stepped into *The Sound of Music*, $5 a day was a very manageable budget.

"Alan, peel me a grape!" Marty said as she leaned back on the grass.

I threw one in her mouth. "It's okay to eat the skin."

"Lazy ass."

Karl had taken out a sketch pad and was scribbling. "What the heck are you drawing?" I asked.

"You three bozos. Stay in those position so I can capture them."

"For how long?" Susan asked.

"Just a few more hours." Karl stood up excitedly. "Just kidding. Wait for it …" He turned over his sketch pad and there were three stick figures holding hands. Wild applause.

"Hey, I've got a question for all of you. What is the one travel experience that stands out as the best – or worst – you have ever experienced when you were little?" Marty asked.

Karl said, "Is there a a prize for the best or worst?"

"Yes." Marty thought for a minute. Then she reached in the picnic basket. "This beautiful piece of brie with your name carved in the skin suitable for mounting!"

Karl huffed.

"I'm not sure that it's something that is special enough for Karl." I said.

"Hey, I mounted one the other day."

"Oh gross, Karl. Just tell me a good travel story."

"Okay. Here's mine. When Karen and I were still married and the girls were still little they really wanted to go to Disneyland. I had a beat up VW bus and we were living in New Jersey. The drive to California would take about a week or so and with that bus, maybe not even make it. Besides, we couldn't afford the gate costs for a family of four, so Karen sewed a couple of costumes like Mickey, Minnie, Goofy and Donald. We headed to Atlantic City, put on the costumes and told the girls we were in Disneyland. Had a great time. They didn't know the difference."

"Who was Goofy?"

"Who do you think, Handler?"

"Very clever, Karl. I could just see you guys walking around Atlantic City in those costumes," Marty said. "Well … MY favorite trip was when I was about seven I think and we went to Worthington, Ohio to the Worthington Doll Museum. There were thousands of dolls from all over the world."

"Oh, man. You win. That's got to be the worst vacation ever." I said.

"At least the scariest." Karl added.

"It was wonderful!" Marty said. "Actually, I didn't care as much about the museum as I did the gift shop. I liked it much better. The dolls were so much cuter." Marty laughed at herself. "How about you, Handler?"

"Well. We didn't ever really go anywhere except a hotel in Biloxi, Mississippi." I said. "Every time we went I had fun I guess. One year there was a hurricane and we still went. I don't think my dad even noticed. I guess we could get the prize for the dumbest vacation. We were stuck there for days. Kinda exciting, though."

"Scary," Susan added. "I went to a math competition in Cleveland one year."

All of us together said. "THE WINNER!"

I really missed those guys when summer hit.

Writing part of the first draft of my novel got a lot of attention the first few weeks however and that felt good. Karol was quickly becoming a memory and my letters to her slowed to one a week.

Barry and Isabel and their kids visited for a week in June. It was great to see them. Barry and I spent a couple of days cranking out some great materials for our game. Funny, I always said program when I talked about it in the past as if game lessened its importance, but that's what it was and that's why the kids loved it: because they were having fun playing it while learning valuable skills.

We were able to construct an actual game board that could be personalized by player and they could track their progress on a timeline that became a Gantt chart for project management. Whether it was a construction project like building a house or a store or planning an event like a wedding or a trial or even a party, they could use the chart to keep them on track. The mechanics really fell on Barry or me (mostly Barry) to initialize, but once they were in place it was pretty easy to keep up.

Figuring out the way we were going to sell this thing was the real challenge. Barry and I disagreed on the ultimate customer. I said the student and he said the teacher. We were both right of course, but we both agreed that the real customer was the school. They would make the purchase because this wasn't a retail product. Kids weren't gonna play this at home – at least not yet.

We had fun designing the graphics. Barry thought that for the next phase, he could take it to his students and let them decide if they thought it was "cool enough" to work.

"I see what you mean about this place, Handler." Barry finished off his beer. We were sitting on long benches outside at the Gasthaus down the street from my place. "It would be a great place to hang for a few years."

"You'd love the students, too. They are so smart. Scary smart." I thought about Becky and Amanda for a microsecond, "and mature beyond their years. Which is not always a good thing."

"You happy, Handler?"

"Sure. I'm not sure where I will be tomorrow or what I'm gonna be doing when I get there, but I don't really care about that right now."

"I envy you. I always know where I will be. And it's not nearly as exciting as this."

"But that's what I envy about you," I said as I toasted him with his empty class. "You've got a family that loves you and you love them. You always know where you'll be. And it's always with them."

Shannon Gallagher left a message for me at READInc. I called her on a Wednesday, after all my buddies had scattered and Barry and Isabel headed to London with their kids. "Is this the world famous Shannon Gallagher?"

"Hardly," she giggled.

"It's not Shannon Gallagher?"

"No, I mean yes. You know what I mean. Not world famous." She hesitated. "You know, Alan, I'm out of practice with you."

"Well. Maybe we should remedy that."

"Maybe we should. What are you doing on June 26th through 28th?" Pretty direct for Shannon, I thought to myself.

"I just checked with my social secretary and was told that I am free!"

"So I have a deal for you. How would you like to come to Rome – all expenses paid by my family – and be my date for my sister's wedding? Before you answer that, I realized that I put you in a tricky position because I asked if you were free before I told you what it was for and if you don't want to come, I would understand because ..."

"Whoa, Gallagher. I'll be there. No need to up-sell."

" ... you might not be a wedding guy."

She spoke over my sentence and then stopped. "Wait. You said you would come? You're okay with that?"

"Sure. I'd love to. I appreciate you asking. It'll be fun."

"Great! Great. Well, I'll make the arrangements and let you know soon. Okay?"

"Okay."

My hand rested on the receiver for a few minutes after I hung up. Shannon Gallagher. I really WAS happy she called. Weddings were usually something I typically would either say no to or sprint out of as fast as I could. No, this time I really wanted to go. With her.

I sat there realizing that ever since Karol, I haven't had a real date or even been interested in a girl. Having a girlfriend who always had me on edge, questioning where I stood was not a great place to be. Shannon was normal and seemed to really like me. That won't work, will it? I apparently needed a woman who had issues and would always keep me on edge.

What am I doing? This is a weekend date for a wedding, not a marriage proposal.

A year ago, I never would have tried to evaluate this. My relationship with Karol had changed that. As much as I tried, I still had strong feelings for her and I'm sure some of my uneasiness was related to guilt.

What the heck? I was determined to have a good time and shut down my pea brain to let things happen naturally.

S hannon met me at the train station the morning of the 26th. She was right on time. The train was late (of course). She gave me a great big hug when I stepped onto the platform and told me how much this meant to her. "Are you kidding?" I said. "The best-looking woman in Rome asks ME out and you are grateful? I am one happy guy." Dogana caught my eye and I quickly turned back to Shannon.

"I missed you, Handler. Nobody lies better than you. Let's get you to the hotel."

Albergo del Senato was right across the square from the Trevi Fountain. I could throw three coins from my hotel room. What a beautiful place. Dr. Cameron Gallagher (Shannon's 'Daddy') who was head of public health for the American Embassy, was also an investor in the hotel's parent company, from what I gathered. About half the rooms were under his name for the weekend wedding.

The plans included a dinner at the hotel's outdoor restaurant with the immediate family – and me – tonight, then tomorrow's wedding at one of the 600 Catholic Churches and reception nearby. I looked at my sport coat and wondered if at some point in the dinner conversation, one of the Gallaghers would ask me to get back to the kitchen. I turned on the hot shower and moved the sport coat to the hook on the bathroom door to steam out the wrinkles.

S hannon met me in the lobby at five. She quickly ushered me over to one of the big couches. "I just wanted to give you a heads-up on who's at our table before you meet them."

"Should I take notes?"

"No, silly." She sat me down. "You are sitting next to Aunt Rachel, my mother's sister and her daughter Stephanie. They both live in New York. Aunt Rachel can be a little abrasive ... sorry."

"Sorry that she's abrasive or that I'm sitting next to her?"

"Both. Stephanie is sweet. She's at Columbia."

"Okay, I'll just tell them to switch seats."

She playfully punched me in the arm. "On my side, is my nana and papa. You will love them."

A little tiny bald-headed man and his much taller wife spotted Shannon and came over to say hello. "Shannon, how long has it been dear? So good to see you."

"You too, Uncle Sean and Auntie Grace." They kissed and hugged. "This is my friend, Alan Handler."

We greeted each other and exchanged pleasantries.

"Are you two headed over to the dinner now?" Auntie Grace asked.

"We are. We'll be right behind you."

As they walked off, Shannon continued her descriptions, "The other couple is my cousin Denise and her husband Peter."

"So ... What's the story with them?"

Shannon hesitated. "Peter is an old high school boyfriend. He still, well, I think he still has a thing for me. Denise and I have a pretty good relationship, but I haven't seen either of them for a while so I just don't know what to expect. Are you okay with that?"

"As long he doesn't call me out for a duel. This is my only coat and it would be hard to get the blood out."

"I think you're safe." She kissed me on the cheek.

S hannon's family filled every table in the restaurant. It was just she and her sister in her immediate family, but there were lots of aunts and uncles and cousins in the extended family. Shannon's sister Katherine had similar features and both girls looked just like their mother Joanne. All were natural beauties. Katherine sat at the table adjacent to us with her parents and the groom, Robert Pierce, and his parents.

Aunt Rachel was true to her characterization. "So, Alvin?"

"Alan." I corrected her.

"Yes, Alan ... how long have you and Shannon dated?"

Shannon jumped in to protect me. "Aunt Rachel, Alan and I are friends. We worked together at Marymount."

"Well, have you slept with him yet?"

I jumped right in. Couldn't help myself. "Absolutely. For about three years now."

"And you're not dating?" Aunt Rachel gasped.

"Oh Lord," Shannon said. "Alan is joking with you."

I noticed just then that ex-boyfriend Peter must have heard the exchange and got up from his seat to greet me. This was going to be a fun night. "I just wanted to introduce myself. Alan. I'm Peter Smith. Shannon and I have a, well, long history."

"Hi Peter. I bet you guys dated in high school. Am I right?" Shannon rolled her eyes.

"Yes! Yes we did. Did Shannon tell you about me?"

"No." I smiled broadly.

Papa Gallagher leaned in and asked Nana, "Is that Alvin boy married to our little Shannon, Mother?"

Nana said, "No, dear. They are just sleeping together."

"Oh. That's nice," Papa said.

Shannon jumped up and addressed our table."Would you all excuse us for a few minutes? I'm going to introduce Alan to some of the family."

She reached under my arm and wrenched me out of my seat as I was just about to bite down on a shrimp from my shrimp cocktail. "Who should we talk to next, Shannon?" I managed to say as I was quickly pulled from our table.

"Alan. You are not helping matters. My family doesn't have a great sense of humor. You can't tease with them."

"I disagree. I think they are a riot. I'm having a great time teasing them."

We landed at the bride's table. Shannon made the rounds and introduced me to her Mommy and Daddy and her sister and husband to be. "Alan, thank you for coming." Joanne said. "We are so glad to meet you."

"Thank you, Mrs. Gallagher. I am honored to be here and to have the pleasure to escort your sister Shannon."

"You charmer. My DAUGHTER Shannon is happy you're here too, It's all she could talk about."

Shannon jumped in. "Well, I was happy you were coming.

Not ALL I talked about. This is Katherine's weekend."

I smiled. "Katherine, you look beautiful."

"Thanks, Alan. You have great taste too."

Dr. Gallagher stood. "Alan, will you join me at the bar for a drink?"

"Sure. Can we get anything for anyone?" Hearing nothing, Dr. Gallagher led me to the other end of the room and we sat at the bar.

He ordered two whiskeys and we toasted to the family. "So Alan, Shannon told me you two work together. Is that right?"

"Yes, sir. Well, we did work together. I was on assignment at Marymount for a couple of months. I live in Vienna now."

"Teaching?"

"Yes. At the American International School,"

"Fine place. Bill Neil still in charge there?"

"He is. Do you know him?"

"I do. You know I was at the Embassy in Vienna for a short period of time years ago. In fact, Shannon went to school there for a while."

"She told me that. You have lived an exciting and interesting life, Dr. Gallagher. Living in Vienna and Rome. "

"I have been blessed, son. I have a wonderful family too. That's key to happiness and success. My daughters are the light of my life."

"Well, you did a great job with Shannon, sir. She is a wonderful girl. I have really enjoyed getting to know her."

Cameron Gallagher studied me for a minute and smiled. I was sure that this was why he was so successful in the diplomatic corps. He was interviewing me without really interviewing me. I would bet he had a file on me in his office and studied it before he met me. But I was at ease with him. He didn't pressure me or ask any embarrassing questions. At least not up to this point. "Well, let's get back to the table. I think I have to give a speech or something. How about that? I pick up the bill and they still make me work."

Shannon and I strolled through the square and down the street after dinner. "Was it awful, Alan?"

I stopped and turned her toward me. "Awful? Heck no. It was really fun. Your family is very cool, Shannon."

"Oh, right. My nosey aunt and my lovesick ex-boyfriend and everybody asking you tons of questions."

"It's because they care about you. Hey, my family's pretty much gone now. I would kill to have a big family like yours. Even your nana and papa are still around."

"Oh yeah, ALVIN."

We both laughed. I stared at her in the light of the street lamps. When her head fell back in laughter, I reached behind her neck and held her. I asked her, "Shannon, do friends kiss?"

She smiled and said, "This friend does."

The first real kiss. Nothing like the first real kiss.

We overslept the next morning. I hadn't slept that soundly in God knows how long. Shannon leaped out of bed a little panicked because of her wedding responsibilities but made it to the church in plenty of time. I followed a little later.

The church was massive: Chelsea Rettoria Santi Vincenzo e Anastasio a fontana di Trevi. I guess the name has to reflect the massiveness as well. My guess was that the churchgoers called it St. Vincent's, but Americans abbreviate everything, so I was probably wrong.

The size of the wedding matched the size of the church. I'm not sure what I was expecting. But it wasn't the enormity of the guest list. I think I was expecting a quaint wedding with the little bells and handful of townspeople. There were more priests than I've ever seen together since they named the new pope. Cameron Gallagher was obviously a big deal in Rome and very well respected.

Shannon and I made a beeline back to the room after the wedding and right before the reception. The rest of that day was fuzzy because I only remember details of what happened in our hotel room that day.

And that will remain secure.

I stayed longer than I had planned in Rome. Shannon lived with a roommate who fortunately traveled back to the states for the summer; so she and I had lots of time to get to know each other.

She was an amazing tour guide … not only for Rome but the rest of Italy and England and France (which we visited over the next month). We spent a few days on the Isle of Capri and saw the Blue Grotto: caves where the water is luminescent blue because of the way the light hits from the opening and below. Capri is built on steep cliffs. We stopped in Florence and saw the well-endowed David statue and then on to Venice to navigate the canals.

London was a musical trip. I wanted to go everywhere the Beatles had been from Abbey Road to Liverpool. Paul's house, John's house. Ringo … I was the ugly American!

Paris was memorable because I got food poisoning. I'm sure it was memorable to Shannon for the same reason. She had to take care of me. I think it was the breakfast. The eggs were runny and undercooked that morning. As we walked the city, I started to feel a little shaky but kept going. That night I managed to get the last two tickets at the music hall for Woody Allen and the Dukes of Dixieland Band. He was touring with them and it was the last stop they would make. As luck would have it, our seats were high above in the rafters. The concert was great, but I felt like I was going to fall to my death, I was so shaky.

That night was the sickest I've ever been. I was in the bathroom for probably eight hours and poor Shannon had to stand by me. We spent another day in the hotel and then a sketchy train ride back to her place in Rome trying not to ... well, you know.

It was really hard to leave Rome and get back to Vienna before the start of fall semester. Shannon had started her lesson planning and we both swore to keep in touch.

Bill Neil had called me and asked me to come to his office. He wanted to talk to me about an assignment. "Alan, you know Kofi Amin?"

"I do. He teaches middle school social studies right?"

"That's right." Bill moved behind his desk and sat down. He folded his arms. "Kofi had a serious automobile accident on the Autobahn while on holiday."

"Oh my God. How serious?"

"Well, serious enough that he's been hospitalized and

still unconscious. It's touch and go. In fact, I'm headed there in just a few minutes."

I slumped in my chair. "Please tell him he's in my thoughts."

"I will." He uncrossed his arms. "I need you to take over one of his sections if you would."

"Of course. I'll do my best."

"It's a mini course in Japanese history. Can you teach Japanese history?"

"Absolutely." I had no clue about Japanese history or how I was going to teach it. But I figured I would give it a shot. How could I say no?

I left Bill's office and headed straight to the Japanese Embassy. Fortunately, information on Japanese life, customs and history was plentiful ... and compartmentalized. Each component had its own brochure: Origami (paper folding), The Royal Family, Geisha, Wars, Foods ... you name it, there was a brochure on it.

That gave me a great idea.

On the first day of class, I came armed with all my brochures. I laid them all out on the back table and waited for my class to arrive. As they started to come in, they cautiously eyed me and then they eyed the table.

When they got settled I began, "Good morning, my name is Mr. Handler and I'll be your teacher for this section of social studies for Mr. Amin." There were murmurs of surprise. Apparently, most of the students were unaware of the circumstances for Mr. Amin's absence. "The reason for that, as some might know but most do not, I'm afraid, is that Mr.

Amin had a car accident on the highway coming back from holiday."

Now there were more murmurs and some were tearing up. One female student raised her hand meekly. "Is Mr. Amin going to be okay?"

"I wish I knew the answer to that. Right now he's in the hospital and he is getting very good care." I noticed that the girl who asked the question was starting to cry. "And what is your name?"

"Sally Kleinfeldt," she managed to say through her tears.

"Well, Miss Kleinfeldt, I know he would love to hear from you and all of your classmates so one of the things we can do today is write get-well cards to Mr. Amin and tell him how much we miss him. Does that sound like a good idea?"

Sally nodded her approval and dried her eyes.

"Good. Now another thing I wanted to do today is introduce what we are studying this term: Japanese history." I walked to the back table. "You may have noticed that I placed a number of brochures on the table. They all relate to Japanese life. And I came up with a plan for all of us to learn as much as we can about the Japanese culture." I reached down and spread the brochures out randomly. "I want each one of you to come to the back table, close your eyes and pick up a brochure."

I called each one up by name and they told me a little about themselves and then randomly picked a brochure.

The first one up was Frankie Hollister, who loved hockey. He closed his eyes and picked up a brochure and when he read it he yelled out, "COOL! I got Samurai!"

"That's great, Frankie. Okay, who's next?" All the hands went up and we were off to a great start. I was glad Frankie picked something that got him excited. Some liked their choices and others weren't thrilled. But overall it piqued their interest.

As everyone studied their brochures I said, "Now, here's what we are going to do with those. Each one of you is going to study your topic and I'll assign you a special day that you will teach class. That's right: You will teach the class about your topic. Like Frankie. He will cover samurai warriors. He might even dress like one that day or draw a warrior or whatever creative thing he can think of. And we will all take notes. Me too! At the end of the term, I'll test you on what you have learned and I think we can have fun with it. Agreed?"

Overwhelming support.

I shared my Japanese history experiment with Susan and Marty. They loved it. They were back from their travels, so we also shared our summer vacation stories. They were all over me about Shannon. They wanted to know everything. The Broadway play *Grease* just came out and all I could think of was that song "Summer Nights": "Tell me more, tell me more..." I told them about the wedding and food poisoning but just kept it at the Cliff's Notes level.

They shared everything. Well, almost.

There was a guy in Amsterdam who took them to a weird party and somehow neither of them remember any details. But they woke up in different beds the next day.

"That's convenient. Neither of you remembers anything?"

"Well, you apparently don't remember details either." Marty said.

"Oh, I remember. I just don't kiss and tell."

"You kissed?"

"Geez."

They asked me about Karl and I told them that I had just gotten a long letter about life in Florida. True to form, he found a flea market that he liked so much that he bought all his clothes and school supplies there – along with pocket watch or two. He was living in a small place on the beach with a female tugboat captain. Karl met her one night in a local bar and she told him about life as a tugboat captain, which is a profession that you have to be born into, apparently. It's handed down from generation to generation with the family tug boat license. She was the first female to have that honor in her family.

The next couple of months seemed like they just sailed by. My Japanese social studies class was a big success. Well, at least I think so: I learned a lot! I talked to Shannon often and we spent many weekends together either at my place or hers. Barry was making great progress with Community, and our plans to move ahead were on full speed.

It was right about the time that I was planning my next career move that I got the call.

"Is this Alan Handler?" The voice on the other end was unfamiliar, I thought, as I stood in the hallway of my apartment.

"Yes. Who's this?"

"This is Sarah Warren." She hesitated. "Sarah Ballard Warren. I'm Karol Ballard's mother, Mr. Handler."

I stood very still. I thought if I moved my feet, I might fall over. "Mrs. Ballard ... Warren. Nice to hear from you."

"I hope you don't mind my call. Karol asked me to reach out to you."

"She did?"

"Yes. She wanted me to ask you if you would come to Meridian."

I hesitated. "I'm just about to wrap up things here in Vienna and I haven't decided on my travel plans."

"I wouldn't want this to be an imposition. But it would be wonderful if you could swing by here."

"Well, I guess I could see about getting a flight in the next week or so ..."

I could hear a flick as she lit a cigarette. "Any time."

FOR THOSE WHO CAN

CHAPTER SEVEN

The Visit to Meridian

The temperature was about 85, but the heat index had to be 100 and I was feeling it. The sweat was pouring down my back even sitting in my air-conditioned rental car. New Orleans was always like this in the hot months, too. You'd think I would have been used to it by now.

I think the discomfort and uncertainty of walking into Karol's mother's house was making it equally difficult. The conversation we had on the phone was a strange one, although not totally unexpected from how many of my conversations with Karol had been in the past ... when we did have conversations.

Sarah Warren's house was nestled in a little rural part of Meridian, on the outskirts of town. No wonder I couldn't find her when I searched in the past, I thought. She didn't use Ballard as her last name. Not surprisingly, Karol never told me, but we rarely talked about her mother.

I pulled up to the front and sat in the car for a few minutes checking the address she gave me with the numbers on the mailbox. Satisfied, I took a deep breath and I walked to the big red door and knocked.

"You must be Alan," an older version of Karol greeted me and warmly took my hand. "Come in. Come in." She ushered me into the living room. It was small but very comfortable. Mrs. Warren handed me a tall glass of lemonade. "You like lemonade?"

"Thanks. It's a real scorcher out there."

"Always, these days." We both sipped our lemonade and smiled at each other. I looked around, waiting for Karol to appear. "Alan, thanks for making the trip down here. I so appreciate it."

"No problem. Is Karol joining us?"

"No she's not, Alan." She paused and wiped a teardrop from her eyes. "Karol passed away two weeks ago."

"What?" I put down my glass right before it almost slipped out of my hand. My heart literally skipped a few beats and I felt a my pulse beat uncontrollably.

"I wanted to meet you in person to tell you this. Karol asked me to call you as well. You meant the world to her."

I could barely speak. "No. This can't be ... What happened? I had no idea ..."

"Of course not. She didn't want you to know about her illness. That's why she came home." Sarah Warren moved over to the couch I was sitting in and sat next to me and held my hand. "You see, Karol was diagnosed a couple of years ago with depression and anxiety that even led to delusional behavior. The doctors tried many different medicines to control these symptoms. But they just got worse. Last year, we took her to the Mayo Clinic and they found the real reason for these symptoms. It wasn't a mental disorder at all. It was a brain tumor."

"And that was causing all these personalty changes?"

"Correct. Neuropsychiatric symptoms they called them."

"She mentioned that Kelly had similar symptoms too."

"Karol is our only child, Alan. Kelly was a way for her to project her pain and her problems into another person."

My God. I felt like I was in some kind of alternate universe. "But she seemed so ... so ..."

"Normal? Until she wasn't?"

I shook my head. "Yes."

"When the doctors found the tumor, they treated it with radiation therapy and that worked to shrink it ... for a time. Karol hated the treatments but was feeling more clarity and left home to go to New Orleans. I was against it. I was devastated. I called her every day, begging her to come home because I knew she wasn't well and needed more care. She would come home for a few days and then back again. You know. You were probably wondering why."

My mind was reeling as I was remembering all our conversations about her mother calling to help out Kelly and her trips back and forth. For him, not her.

Her mother started to cry. "The last visit home ... she ... was very very sick ..."

"Why didn't they operate on her."

"The tumor was in a place in the brain that they couldn't remove. Even Mayo said it was inoperable."

"I wish I would have known. I would have been there or here."

"She didn't want you to know. She didn't want you to see her like that. I know she wanted to start writing you and

I even helped her with the first letter." Sarah handed me a sealed envelope.

"This was her second letter. She wanted you to have it when she passed."

I opened it carefully.

Dearest Handler

Don't be sad for me. Well, maybe for a day.

But that's it.

I'm so sorry that I didn't tell you everything but you know why. I don't want to be remembered shriveled up and unable to walk. I want you to remember me as a kick ass woman who was fun and was crazy and was in your life for a short time but filled all the spaces.

That's how I'll remember you.

Make me a promise…

Go to O'Malley's in South Bend and sit at the bar and have a beer for me. Then crank up Ernie K-Doe and play "There's a Certain Girl" real loud.

That's where I'll be.

Always

Karol

I could feel the tears well up in my eyes as Sarah brought out a shoebox filled with my letters. "I know she read most of them before she fell into a coma … Alan…" She held my hand tightly.

"… there's something else …"

FOR THOSE WHO CAN

EPILOGUE

Jake Finds the Answers

Jake searched for the next page of the manuscript. "It ended with there's something else?" He thought to himself. "What else was there? It can't end that way! Emory Ohlmstead had said it was an unfinished manuscript. He must know the rest of the story."

Jake started to call Emory but his phone buzzed before he dialed.

It was his ex-wife, Emma. He put it down without answering it. He glanced at Emma's face from a shelf across the room. She looked at him so sweetly ... as did his daughter Hannah, a freshman at Ohio State. Neither had much use for him any more. Jake really couldn't blame them. Emma was probably looking for the divorce paperwork.

He couldn't think about that now. It was time to finish getting answers for at least this part of his life. He jumped in the shower and packed quickly.

Emory Ohlmstead's office was not what Jake was expecting. It was still where it was 50 years ago. The original South Bend building had been renovated many times but it still retained the same charm that the original had. It was still like going over to someone's house for a visit.

"Jake, what a nice surprise." Emory greeted him with outstretched arms.

"Mr. Ohlmstead. Thanks for seeing me on short notice."

"It's Emory. And I was happy to make time for you, my boy. I see you have the manuscript with you. Did you read it?"

Jake had carried it under his arm and laid it down on the coffee table. "I did. I couldn't stop reading it ... until I HAD to."

Emory smiled. "Unfinished. I warned you."

"You know what happened next, don't you?"

"I do."

"Then why on earth didn't you tell me?"

"Well ... because you had to read this first."

"Okay. I did. SO ???"

"Sit down Jake." Jake pulled out a chair. Emory sat across for him. "So ... After Sarah Warren said that there was more, she drove Alan to the hospital where Karol spent her last days. She took him into the hospital's Neonatal Intensive Care Unit and introduced him to a tiny, fragile baby who had tubes and wires sticking out of every place on his little body."

"Wait. You're saying ..."

"That's right. Karol was pregnant when she came home the last time ... with Alan's baby. Karol insisted on carrying the baby full term even though her own outcome was doubtful and the baby might not survive. The baby was born as Karol slipped into a coma but before she did, she told her mother that she wanted to let your dad know." Emory paced the office.

"Your dad decided that day to move to Meridian, Mississippi where he started his first real novel and raised that little boy with Sarah's help until he convinced Shannon to join him and they were married the following year."

"So let me get this straight. That baby is a brother I never knew I had?"

"No, Jake." Emory sat across from him. "That baby was you."

"Me?" Jake looked at Emory confused and almost angry. "That can't be, Emory."

"Oh, but it is, my boy." Emory pulled out a big manila envelope with Jake's name on it. He opened it and handed Jake paperwork. Here is your birth certificate, paperwork that changed your name from Baby Boy Ballard to Jacob Emory Handler and a few other things of your father's that are now yours."

Emory put his arm around Jake. "I know this is going to take some time to get your arms around, but I want you to know that I knew both your natural mother and your mother who raised you. They loved you and your dad very much."

"Why didn't he tell me?"

"I think he felt that he would spare you the pain and protect you and love you until you were old enough and then … well … time gets away from you and when he did write his manuscript, he ran out of time."

Jake reached into the envelope and pulled out a thick document with the corporate brand he was very familiar with … Community.

"Oh. That one you'll want to study, my boy."

"I helped Dad with a few things he needed a couple of

years ago when I worked for City Planning. Just some IT stuff, but he seemed pleased."

"I know he was." Emory said.

J ake sat at O'Malley's Bar, nursing his Dewar's and water. He opened the manila envelope and reached in. There were a handful of pictures. Many were different views of a burned-out Buick and one of a smiling group of people that toasted the camera ... Alan, Emory, a young Barry and Isabel and one he didn't recognize. Maybe that was Karol, he thought.

The bartender happened to glance down at the picture. "Ha! That's something! That picture was taken right here. Right in the seats you're sitting in – must be 40 years ago."

"Fifty," Jake said, and smiled.

Jake pulled out the Community document and opened the cover folder. There was a recent magazine folded to a marked page with a sticky note. It was a story with a picture of Alan in graduation regalia on stage giving an address. Jake scanned the article. The magazine was from LSU, Alan's alumni mater. Alan was delivering the graduation address after receiving an honorary doctorate degree. There was a marked passage which read:

"... I am so pleased to have been given this honor. There are so many people who have been responsible for so much of my success in everything I have accomplished. As graduates, I am certain that you too have much to be thankful for and many to thank for where you are today.

"When my partner Barry Myers and I started our company, Community, we never really knew what to expect, but the overwhelming response we received pushed us forward. We were able to bring the Community into the classroom. I'm happy to announce that in the coming months we will be introducing software that will bring the classroom into the Community as well. It was developed by my son, Jacob Handler, whose brilliant vision will take us to the next level ..."

The sticky note simply read ... "send to Jake, my one and only (with a little Superman logo that Alan had drawn)."

At the very bottom of the envelope was a tiny baby bracelet that was small enough to be a ring. It spelled out J-A-C-O-B in tiny blocks. Jake squeezed it in his hand and started to cry.

His phone buzzed. It was Emma. He managed to get one word out when he answered, "Hi."

"Hey," Emma said. "Jake, I just heard about your dad. I wish you would have told Hannah and me. Are you okay?"

"Not really, Emma ..." The tears were now running down his face. He could barely speak. "... I'm just a few miles outside of Chicago ... in South Bend ... I really would love to ... Can I ... maybe buy you ... dinner?"

"No," Emma replied.

Jake hesitated, then answered, "I ... I understand."

"Come over to the house. I'll cook."

END

About the Author...

When Joel Momberg wasn't pounding out a mean New Orleans-flavored boogie-woogie on the nearest piano, he was setting the tone as Chief Executive Officer for the University of South Florida Foundation. But Momberg's hands have done far more than shape the historic direction of the recently completed billion-dollar USF Unstoppable Campaign, or build All Children's Hospital into a community treasure during his 30 years in executive leadership positions – helping create iconic events such as the Children's Miracle Network Telethon, the Taste of Pinellas and Regional Emmy-winning children's music.

Recently, those hands have been busy working the keyboard of his trusty laptop to produce his latest novel, *For Those Who Can*. This follows his second novel, *Sammy*, a lively and unique mystery set in his native New Orleans. and his 2013 debut novel, *Home Movies*, a whodunit that unfolds on the familiar territory of St. Pete Beach. The books draw from Momberg's rich life experience with engaging plot lines and characters from his fertile imagination.

Momberg resides in St. Petersburg with wife Debbie, and has three children – Nicole, Alissa, and Josh – and five grandchildren.

CPSIA information can be obtained
at www.ICGtesting.com
Printed in the USA
BVHW041230171120
593306BV00004BA/7/J